HALF BREED LOVE

Also By Bernadette Lundall

Inner Wisdom and Life Skills [Beginners]
50 Simple Business Ideas To Make Money
Dana and Daddy

Half Breed Love

Published by Bernadette Lundall 2013

ISBN 978-0-9922212-4-9

Printed and bound by CreateSpace, an Amazon.com Company, 2014
This book is in no way endorsed or sponsored by CreateSpace,
Amazon, or their affiliates.

Illustrator Cover: Sacha de Speville

For all the courageous women in my family; your wisdom, strength and endurance has rubbed off onto me.

Chapter One

"You are not serious, Mitch! Do you really expect me to drive 180 kilometers to Robertson just to go and interview some foreigner?" asked Jesse Kearns indignantly. "Yes, I do! And he isn't just any foreigner. Joshua Bolton is making news in South Africa. He is one of the first landowners to formulate the idea of land ownership for his employees," said Mitch Langley. "What do you mean, the master is giving his slaves some land?" retorted Jesse sarcastically. Mitch handed her the file and smiled, "I am your master and I'm ordering you to do this assignment!" he retaliated, walking away. She saluted his back. "I saw that! And don't forget you'll be there for at least a week. I've hired a car for you and you'll be staying at the quaint *Old Village Hotel*. Bring back as much information as possible," he ordered, walking away.

Jesse was glad to be out of the office for a change. She had been working for the Cape Town Post for the last three years and had taken to journalism like a duck to water. Her manager, Mitch Langley had really shown her the ropes and had groomed her to become an excellent journalist. After completing her Bachelor of Technology degree in journalism at the Cape Peninsula University of Technology in Cape Town, she had decided to travel to Britain and Europe. Her travels abroad had helped her to become more independent and more experienced in the ways of the world. She was now able to apply her observation skills more precisely in her work as a journalist at home. However, going abroad for experience was not all that she had hoped for. She had gone especially to England to find someone. *Her father*... A man she only knew from a photograph.

Jesse forced the image of her father out of her mind and concentrated on the road ahead. The N1 freeway snaked ahead of her like a black mamba uncoiling itself as she rode its back. Robertson was at least another one and a half hours drive. She wondered what this Joshua

1

Bolton was like. If he was anything like her father ... When he found out that her mother was pregnant with his child, he hung around for a year and returned to England in haste. Nobody knew why he had left so hurriedly or where he was. He was supposedly so much in love with Jesse's mother. Jesse's mother was half Indian half Nama. The Nama people are the indigenous people of Namibia and North Western South Africa. Being of bi-racial decent, Jesse was exceptionally beautiful. She had a deep bronze tan and was tall with large almond shaped smoky black eyes shrouded by the longest lashes any woman is blessed to be endowed with. She had thick well-formed eyebrows, the cutest little nose and a warm generous mouth. But, her hair was the one feature that made heads turn. She had very curly soft black hair that fell in tendrils down to her waist. However, what made Jesse truly beautiful was her complete unawareness of her own beauty. She had a strange innocence and a naiveté that most people were well intentioned.

Suddenly she was knocked out of her reverie when she saw the signboard reading 'Robertson' R60. She followed the directions and turned left. Once she had reached the highest point in the road, she started her descent and it was an awesome sight. Robertson lay asleep in the valley below. She was now entering wine country. The little town seemed to be only just waking up to the day. She could see many little buildings in the distance shrouded in a light mist desperately hovering above while the sun was doing its best to melt it away. There were also fields that looked freshly ploughed and vineyards seeming to stretch for miles. It was amazing how straight the rows of vines appeared as if the position of each plant was geometrically calculated. As she drove past the vineyards, her eyes were level with the stems of the vines. If she drove slowly enough she could see straight down each row. Jesse imagined playing hide and seek or getting lost in the maze of the vines and trying to find her way back. The air was fresh and crisp and something about the place smelled different. She noticed that there wasn't a rush of traffic and

2

people who drove past her actually waved. This was very new to Jesse. Coming from a busy city like Cape Town, there was no time for friendliness. Looking down at Robertson from the distance she was at, everything seemed to stand still and she relished in the quiet of the moment.

Jacaranda trees lined the main road in Robertson. The purple and lilac Jacaranda flowers hung in heavy masses on the trees and gave the town its unique character. It seemed as though an artist had painted the flowers on the laden trees. The air smelled as though the flowers had sprayed scent down the main road. This beautiful sight before her seemed unreal. Jesse decided to stop at a coffee shop on the corner of the main road in Robertson. She ordered toast and marmalade, her favourite, and a steaming cup of coffee. She began to make some notes on her notepad. She wrote down her observations of what she had already noticed about the buildings, farms and people.

Jesse jotted down some questions in preparation for her interview. She already knew what she was going to ask, however as in this business, it was always better to be prepared from all angles. One never knew how an interview could turn out. "Can you give me directions to a farm called '*Sonder Moeite*' please?" she asked the waitress. The waitress was very obliging and drew the directions on a clean serviette. Jesse thanked her, tucking the serviette carefully into her pocket. She was not even aware of the stares and the heads turning as she left the coffee shop. As she drove, she wondered why this Bolton guy had not changed the name of the farm to its English equivalent. He had kept the Afrikaans name, which meant 'without effort or trouble'

Jesse drove through the town – according to the directions on the serviette. She passed the police station and the library in the main road and almost out of town, she turned left onto a dirt road. This road seemed to wind its way towards the Langeberg Mountains. Jesse drove slowly as there were some sharp hairpin bends and she was unsure of how steep or narrow the road would become ahead of her. She drove through a valley with bluish mountains on one side and dark forests on the other. It was majestic. God's hand had surely been here. Jesse drove very slowly as the road made a few sharp turns. Finally, she reached the farm and slowed down in front of the open gates. Huge emblems embraced the gates with the Afrikaans name *'Sonder Moeite'* in large brass letters. Directly beneath it were little people with hoes also made of brass, symbolically digging the land.

The long driveway leading up to the homestead was lined with Jacaranda trees also heavy with purple and lilac flowers. It was an awesome sight and lent one to believe that the driveway led to some other mystery farther beyond. The Jacaranda trees seemed to be the trademark of Robertson. Ahead of the Jacaranda trees was a vegetable garden. Jesse could see carrot and beetroot tops and large cabbages and tomatoes growing. As she neared the homestead with its beautiful Cape Dutch gables and shuttered windows, she could see a thick vine growing next to the patio with its large leaves covering the overhead beams forming a shady green roof over the patio. It was truly a beautiful home. The ostentatious roses on either side of the main steps gave the house a somewhat feminine touch.

Jesse climbed up the front steps and knocked on the huge brass knocker. She heard footsteps on hollow wooden floors. A housekeeper appeared wearing a starched white apron. "Good afternoon, I'm here to see Mr Joshua Bolton", she said. "Mr Bolton is still in the vineyards. He will be back for lunch, which is only in about ten minutes. You are welcome to wait in the living room," said the housekeeper. "Thank you, I will wait, as I've driven from Cape Town." She did not seem perturbed that Jesse had come such a long way. The housekeeper showed Jesse into a large room with a huge brown leather sofa and various odd chairs. Everything seemed antique and expensive. The room had a formidable aura of history with paintings hanging on the walls. The high-embossed ceilings and the wooden floors spoke of a time long passed and a culture almost forgotten. There was no particular theme or style to the room – not that she would have recognized any décor style - but it seemed very comfortable and lived in. Above the wooden and mosaic tiled fireplace was an enormous painting with different shades of red and brown. Jesse couldn't exactly make out what it was supposed to be. There were some magazines and newspapers on the coffee table and she glanced at them while she waited.

Soon she heard voices outside. She heard one Afrikaans accent and one unmistakable British accent. She could hear them loud and clear. The voices were debating whether they should harvest the grapes on or before the end of the week. Jesse sat up straight and prepared herself to meet her interviewee. Joshua Bolton came marching into the house. His footsteps were so loud on the hollow wooden floors that he sounded like a giant entering his castle. Images of Jack and the Beanstalk flashed through her mind and in an instant, he stood before her. She got up slowly taking in this picture of manhood. He was not at all, what she had expected. Joshua Bolton had jet-black straight hair cropped short and the most stunning hazel eyes she had ever seen. He had a tan that she thought any British man couldn't have achieved naturally. He was tall and lithe and his legs were long and muscular, stretching within his jeans. The sunlight streamed through the wide windows and lit his jet-black hair making it gleam almost purple. His entire demeanor reeked of money. He looked as though he couldn't be bothered with the small things in life. The lure of big expensive developments energized his attention. He looked hot and irritated and seemed perturbed that she had come at such an awkward time. "Can I help you?" he breathed agitatedly. She noticed immediately that he had a dimple on one cheek. How cute or odd Jesse thought. "I'm Jesse Kearns, from the Cape Town Post. I'd like to interview you about the concept of employee land ownership as opposed to land redistribution which the government is currently trying to get under way," she responded stretching out her hand. "Really!" he sneered.

"Mr. Bolton, if this is a bad time…" "Josh! It's not a bad time. Your manager did call to arrange this appointment," he added changing his tactic. "Allow me to freshen up and we can talk over lunch." He turned around and walked out before she could respond. Something about him seemed wicked. She wondered if it was that dimple on his cheek. His arrogance left her feeling slightly defensive. His presence seemed to have invaded her mind. She knew instinctively that this was going to be a difficult interview. However, thanks to her training, she came prepared for almost anything. Jesse settled back into the leather sofa and took a magazine paging through it absent-mindedly wondering what made the owner of *Sonder Moeite* tick.

He returned shortly and escorted her into the dining area. She could smell his aftershave and his presence seemed to envelope her as he walked close behind her into the dining area. The dining room was narrow and long with heavy cream and gold taffeta drapes extending to the floor. Close to the entrance of the dining room stood a heavy sideboard definitely from the Cape Dutch period. Antique collectors' plates lined the top shelves. There was a long heavy looking Mahogany table in the centre of the room with twelve chairs clamoring around it. There were just two settings, one at the head of the table and the other to the side. He pulled the chair to the side out for her and made sure that she was comfortably seated, before he took his place at the head of the table. 'Where else would he sit,' she thought. The food was warm and comforting and reminded her of her own mother's cooking. He passed the dishes to her in silence and they both dished their food. A slight discomfort seemed to creep up Jesse's spine. She was never one to ignore her sixth sense. She could not help wondering if this was a mistake. "So what exactly is it that you want to know about *Sonder Moeite*?" he muttered breaking the silence. He had scarcely said the words '*Sonder Moeite*' when she had to bite her lip to prevent herself from laughing. His English accent sounded so out of place saying an Afrikaans name. In fact, he sounded ridiculous to her and she wondered why he hadn't changed his farms' name to something more pronounceable for himself. "Well," she said trying not to let on that she found him strangely funny, "how did you come up with the idea of giving your workers ownership of your land and how is it working for you?" "I am a major shareholder, I own 51% of the land and my workers own 49%. That way I'm sure I won't be bothered with labour disputes, strikes or theft. It's unlikely that any logical person would steal from themselves and withholding labour means that the workers own profits will be directly affected." His voice was deep and gruff and he almost came across as though what he was saying was the most natural thing in world economics. Jesse was impressed, he seemed so knowledgeable and articulate. "But where did they get the money to purchase their share of the land?" she persisted curiously. "The government and wine farmers put their heads together and formed a wine co-operative where workers could participate in the rural economy of this country. I believe that the sponsorship of workers to participate in the economy is the only way to boost the growth of the rural economy as well as solve the problem of poverty," he said watching her intently. "So do workers have to repay these sponsored loans?" she enquired. "No, because the government is investing in people and benefiting economically as well." He enraptured her with his knowledge and ingenuity. Then suddenly his train of thought changed... "But why did you really come here Ms Kearns?" he demanded. "I beg your pardon?" She was completely surprised and caught off guard by his change of attitude. "You heard me", he growled darkly. "The real reason you are here!" She noticed that his clenched jaw was pulsating. "I told you, the Cape Town Post is doing a series of articles on the question of land redistribution and how it affects farm owners, workers and claimants," she added, confused by his implications. "You do know that many people suffered under *Apartheid* laws and were forcibly removed from their land," she challenged. "I am well aware of the history of this country," he returned. "I'd also like to interview some of your other shareholders, if I may?" Josh got up abruptly without answering her question. "This meeting is over Ms Kearns." He stressed the *Ms* part of her title. "I have other more important matters to attend to and I'm sure you can see yourself out." He strode out of the room without waiting for a response from Jesse.

Jesse stared at his back in astonishment. What on earth just happened here, she thought to herself. She got up slowly, thinking quickly. 'Okay, I'm old enough to know that that wasn't personal. Hell, he doesn't even know me! Maybe it's the old race demon rearing its ugly head again. What is it with English men?' she thought. 'Well, he certainly isn't going to get away so easily. I didn't drive out all this way for nothing.' She intended to get more interviews and more information for her article. Whether it meant harassing him for more information or hunting down his other shareholders, Jesse intended to go back to Cape Town with lots of valuable information for her article. In any event, Mitch had said that it would take her a week of research. She slipped her hand into her pocket and extracted one of her business cards. Placing the card quietly on the table she walked out casually.

Josh Bolton was completely intoxicated with Jesse Kearns. He had expected a much older plain looking woman. When he saw the young twenty-five year old with her smoky almond eyes and long curly hair he could barely think straight. She had stirred something deep in his loins. Something he hadn't felt in a very long time. But he knew that beauty was only skin-deep and he had to be very careful of Jesse. The press was always just after one thing. Gossip! He had to avoid being on the front-page news at all cost. At least until he had sorted out his personal life. When he went back into the dining area, she had already left but a faint scent of her perfume lingered. He stood behind the chair where she had sat and closed his eyes, deeply inhaling the sweet fragrance of flowers that she left behind. He noticed her business card and picking it up he smiled and pocketed it.

Jesse drove back to town and decided to book into her hotel. She found the *Old Village Hotel* quite easily. It was really a quaint little hotel. There was a very small reception area with framed photographs of important towns' people on the wall. The reception area led straight into a clean white washed living room where there were various cottage styled chairs placed at strategic points in the room. The wooden floors were comparable to the Cape Dutch farm style homesteads. A huge stone fireplace with an assortment of blue and white Chinese pottery pieces on the mantelpiece dominated the room. The living room had a very homely atmosphere. Once she had booked in, the porter carried her bags upstairs to a cozy little suite. The room's walls were a deep yellow. The curtains and the duvet cover were a matching yellow with small little red flowers scattered across them. This was a happy room and Jesse was intent on having a pleasant time in *Robertson* despite Josh Bolton's bad behaviour.

While she unpacked her clothes, she went over in her mind the events of the interview. Joshua Bolton spoke very intelligently about his endeavours. He seemed to come across as one who cared about people, the problem of poverty, world peace and the environment. She went over her questions to him again. Was she too forthright? Perhaps he thought that she was forward. But what did he expect? Mitch had confirmed her appointment with him so he knew that she was coming to interview him. Maybe he was a chauvinist and expecting a male journalist to interview him. Perhaps that was it – he was upset that he had to lower himself down to her female level. The afternoon did not make sense at all. Even his good looks did not make sense. Why would God bestow such good looks on such a jerk?

9

Jesse dined alone that evening. The service was very welcoming and the food was healthy country style cuisine. She had grilled chicken with vegetables and salad. For dessert, which was her favourite part of the meal, she had decadent ice cream strewn with hazelnuts, flaked chocolate and a dollop of whipped cream. Jesse insisted that the waiter pour her sparkling fruit juice into a wine glass. She didn't drink alcohol and she liked to pretend that the sparkling fruit juice was wine that she was drinking. This made her feel more sophisticated. She couldn't understand how people could drink wine; it always tasted like medicine to her. And she wasn't going to pretend to be cultured in that way.

After her meal, Jesse retired upstairs to have a hot foam bath. She lay soaking in the tub playing with the bubbles and wondering what had happened between her and Josh. Again, she went over the days events in her mind. She realized that this was her problem as usual. She would over analyse everything. Aggh! She slid under the water with her head covered with bubbles. As she emerged, she indulged herself anyway. Had she said anything untoward? she thought again. Was she too forceful? His behaviour made no sense to her at all. Perhaps he was used to his 'slaves' bowing down to him and he expected her to be more submissive. He seemed surprised when he first saw her. Perhaps he was expecting a man after all. But she couldn't get him out of her mind. "Yes Mr Bolton, No Mr Bolton!" she mimicked. "You will give me the information I require, you silly farmer!" she said aloud.

Sitting in front of the mirror in her dressing gown, applying her moisturizer, Jesse proceeded to 'interview' Josh Bolton. "So tell me Mr Bolton, oh sorry, Josh," she said sarcastically, "how many slaves do you have on 'Sonder Moeite'?" she deliberately emphasized his British accent. Laughing loudly she continued, "Do you toll the slave bell at four am or at five am? Oh dear me, Mr Bolton, how many of the fair skinned *youngins* are yours?" Jesse stopped laughing at the mirror. She stared back at her own reflection. Why had her father abandoned her as a baby? Why had he refused to acknowledge her existence? Was he so ashamed to have a brown-skinned child? The more she thought of Josh Bolton the more she couldn't stand him.

Jesse decided that after breakfast the following day she would try to interview the neighbouring farmers and ask them what their opinion was about this worker-shareholder concept. Perhaps then, she'd be able to gather more information on the 'Sonder Moeite' farm. Then she'd have more ammunition when she approached Josh Bolton the next day. Jesse went to sleep feeling sure that her strategy for the following day would yield better results for her article.

Chapter Two

Dressed in her white Lycra T-shirt, which emphasized her narrow waist and perky breasts, Jesse pulled on her jeans and brown leather boots. She added a touch of gloss to her lips and stood back looking at herself in the mirror. "Not bad at all Ms Kearns; not bad at all..." she said aloud and left the room with a skip in her step.

She spent the better part of the morning visiting three neighbouring farms. All the farmers were welcoming and invited her in for tea. Most of them were against the workers owning shares in land that they themselves had paid for. But more interestingly, none of them knew anything about Josh Bolton or '*Sonder Moeite*' except that the farm seemed to be flourishing.

Well it was time for Jack to climb up the beanstalk and meet the giant again, she thought. Jesse found herself driving straight up the Jacaranda tree lined driveway once more. This time the housekeeper informed her that Mr Bolton was out on business in town. Jesse decided to take a walk into the vineyards and interview the workers herself. After all, according to Josh, they were also shareholders. The vines glistened with water droplets, having recently been irrigated. She could smell the damp soil and it brought back memories of her grandmother planting vegetables in their back garden. The rows and rows of vines seemed to stretch to the foot of the Langeberg mountain range in the distance. Just by looking at the vine stems, they seemed very old and brittle. She approached the workers who were mostly very friendly and more interested in this city girl than talking about themselves or the farm. "How old are the vines?" enquired Jesse curiously. A female worker responded in Afrikaans, "Sommige van hierdie vingerde is oor die vyftig jaar oud, my kind." [*Some of these vines are over fifty years old, my child*] While one of the farm workers, who appeared to be a foreman, explained how they harvest the grapes, "We have to pick the smaller grapes off the bunch and throw them away because the small unripe grapes prevent the larger ones on the bunch from getting ripe," said Jaco. "We test the grapes by tasting them closer to harvesting time. You see, the small grapes are sour and will spoil…" he suddenly became quiet in mid sentence.

Jesse turned around and looked straight into Josh Bolton's lead face. His face was hard and his angry eyes pierced right through her. It seemed as if the hazel dots in his eyes were shooting out of their usual pattern in his irises. One had to be blind not to notice his steel anger. No wonder Jaco had stopped in mid sentence. Josh was visibly fuming. "What do you think you're doing Ms Kearns!" he bellowed. Before she could answer, he grabbed her by the arm and marched her towards the house. She was completely aware of his hard body pressing against her back. His smell was tantalizing her senses and she felt as though she was being swept away by a wave of confusion. She wanted to fight him but she also wanted to give in to him at the same time. Her senses were going wild. She had to gain control of herself. "What on earth do you think you're doing!" she managed to shriek back at him. "This is private property and you are trespassing!" He pulled her into the house and turned her around to face him. She was very aware of the closeness of their bodies and she could feel his hot breath against her cheek. His hazel eyes blazed furiously down at her and his chest heaved with molten anger. She could scarcely believe that a mere interview could have such an effect on his personality. Jesse's toes curled in her shoes as his behaviour sparked something deep in her pelvis. She turned away flushed, hoping he hadn't noticed anything. She could feel his eyes bearing down on her and a tingling sensation went down her spine. 'This is crazy,' she thought. Turning to face him she said, "You were not in, so I asked the other shareholders to explain the success of this farm or are your slaves not allowed to speak to the press?" she taunted him. In one sweeping movement, he grabbed her arm and pulled her even closer to him. Her legs nearly buckled under her and his breath was so close, tormenting her. Her brain was racing; she had to do something. She couldn't allow him to get the better of her.

13

"You didn't get my permission nor did you follow protocol!" She looked at his hand on her arm and back at him again and asked coolly, "Is this how you treat women in England, Mr Bolton? Because where I come from, this is called abuse!" She wrenched her arm away and marched off before he could say anything. He looked on, as her long dark curls enveloped her body, licking the wind behind her like a hundred Komodo dragon tongues.

It seemed that Jesse Kearns had succeeded in making Josh Bolton look like a fool. But she knew that that was not the end of her encounter with the *major shareholder*. She was aware that she was strangely excited by his anger and her body betrayed her by crying out for more. She felt a sudden powerful rush of adrenaline, as if nothing could touch her when she was able to instigate his temper. The fact that she was capable of making him lose his temper gave her considerable satisfaction.

Josh Bolton was not amused. In fact, he was angrier with himself than with Jesse. How could he have allowed a woman ten years younger than him to get the better of him? He couldn't get her out of his mind. Never before in his life had he lost control of himself, not even with Ava's scandalous tactics. He was used to being in control of himself and others. He clenched and unclenched his fist repeatedly.
He had to see her again. Should he reveal the real reason for his outburst? He decided not to, just in case he read about it in the morning newspaper the following day.

Jesse was tired after the day's events and decided to lie down in her yellow hotel room. Drained of emotion and even too tired to think of her encounter with Josh Bolton, she closed her eyes and drifted off into a deep sleep. She dreamt that she was walking through a vineyard and there was a little blue bird following her. He was singing to her and hopping from vine to vine but whenever she

14

turned around and smiled at him, he would stop chirping. The chirping was very pleasing and happy but she so much wanted to look at the pretty bird. When she turned suddenly to look at him, he disappeared and Josh Bolton stood there fixing her with his unusually penetrating gaze. He came towards her and she stood frozen to the ground. He put his hand behind her neck and pulled her towards him. She floated towards him. His eyes were extraordinarily bright and the hazel colours in his irises were dancing around mocking her. Jesse looked at Josh, saw the corner of his hard mouth twitch, and become softer, revealing that unmistakable dimple in his cheek. He looked despicably handsome. She tried to protest and opened her mouth to say something but the words wouldn't come out. She felt his hot passionate lips on hers, kissing her so tenderly that she wanted to cry. She moaned softly feeling his manhood rise against her body and in the distance,… she heard a telephone ringing… The ringing became persistent and she was jolted out of her dream. The telephone at her bedside was ringing. She answered in a sleepy voice. "Hello, Jesse Kearns." "Did I wake you?" the voice asked mockingly. Jesse was shocked. She sat bolt upright blushing and trying to hide her embarrassment, convinced that he could see her through the telephone. What would Josh think if he knew that just moments earlier he had been kissing her in a dream? "No," she lied feebly, "what do you want?" "Dinner! Tonight! You and I."

"I beg your pardon?" "We need to talk, clear things up," he challenged. He caught her completely off guard. She needed to say something in order to avoid answering the offer. "How did you know I was staying at the *Old Village Hotel?*" "This is a small town Ms Kearns. I'll pick you up at seven pm. Cheers," and the phone clicked off. The man had such a nerve! He hadn't even given her a chance to accept or reject his offer.

Jesse sat on the edge of her bed swinging her legs to and fro wondering what to do next. Should she go or should she not? Well this was one way of continuing her interview. It was established then, this was not a date. This was a continuation of her interview. What should she wear? She became frantic, tearing open the cupboard door and rummaging through her week's clothes. Then she stopped. 'This is ridiculous!' she said to herself. 'It's an interview!' It's not a date so why am I so worried about what Josh Bolton thought of my attire anyway. He was a rude obnoxious man who had no inter-personal skills whatsoever. She would dress to make herself look and feel good. Eventually she settled on a short-sleeved brown wrap-around dress that just barely covered her knees. She could almost hear her grandmother say, *'Never show a man too much skin or he won't appreciate the rest of it when he does see it!'* She smiled fondly and wondered what her grandmother would say about her now if she were still alive. Jesse had a quick shower and got dressed. She took extra care to spray some of her favourite perfume on and added a touch of make up to her lips and eyes. Lastly, she slipped on her brown and khaki wedge heeled sandals where the straps clung tightly to her gorgeous ankles. She stepped back and looked at herself in the mirror. Sometimes she hardly recognized herself. She grabbed her bag and leaving the room, she wondered what the night would have in store for her.

Jesse walked carefully down the stairs with her hair trailing obediently behind her. Josh was already waiting in the foyer and turned to see her coming down the stairs. He held his breath. His eyes followed her glistening legs as she took each step – one at a time. She was exquisite. She was a vision to behold! He had never known any woman to have such an effect on him. "Good evening, Ms Kearns," he spoke casually. "Good evening. Perhaps you should drop the *Ms Kearns* tonight and call me Jesse?" "Alright, Jesse," he emphasized her name with a whimsical smile. That one word sounded like heaven on his lips. Jesse eyed him mischievously. He had on dark pants with a white shirt which was unbuttoned at the neck. Josh looked quite casual but something about the way he dressed and carried himself spoke of money. Jesse noticed that he also wore jewelry. He wore a platinum chain with a medallion and a heavy expensive looking watch. Jesse could not determine the brand but she surely noticed the sparkling diamonds on the watch face. Josh led her to his black German convertible sports car waiting at the curb. Jesse was impressed - she had never pictured him in a sports car. He opened the door gallantly and allowed her to slip into the front passenger seat. The leather smell was overpowering and there were so many dials and buttons in the car that it appeared like a cockpit of an aeroplane. He got in beside her and she turned to smile at him. Perhaps this would be a more pleasant evening after all. Josh turned on the engine and maneuvered the car onto the road with such elegance and precision that she barely realized the car was in motion.

Josh had made reservations at the fancy and exclusive *Pringles* restaurant. Many people seemed to know him and greeted him as they walked to their table. Jesse noticed many women looking jealously at them as they walked past their tables, then turned to one another to gossip. Josh Bolton must be one of the most eligible bachelors in Robertson. A waiter brought the menus as soon as they were seated, and asked Josh what they would be drinking. "How about champagne for the lady?" he asked Jesse. "I don't drink", she mumbled flatly, feeling terribly insecure and unsophisticated, "and we certainly don't have anything to celebrate now do we?" she added trying to divert the attention from her refusal to drink. "That's okay. The champagne of fruit juices then and a dry white wine please," he said to the waiter, ignoring her comment .The waiter knew exactly what he was talking about and disappeared to fetch their drinks. "So, the tough reporter is beginning to reveal herself," Josh remarked sardonically. Suddenly Jesse felt shy and defensive. "I don't like the taste of alcohol and I'm certainly not going to drink to impress you." Josh held his hands up in mock defense, "The lady doth protest too much!" Just then, they were served with delicious appetizers and Jesse decided to see where the conversation was going. "So which

17

part of England are you from?" she asked curiously. "Cornwall. My family has an estate there." "Oh, don't tell me your family has a vineyard?" "Oh no, horses!" he said emphatically. "My brother Nico and my father breed horses and run an equestrian training school. I have a sister, Isabella who is a fashion designer somewhere in New York but we never get to see her. My dear mother stays at home and tries to manage everybody's lives," he answered jokingly. He had given Jesse a load of information without her having asked. "Do you miss Cornwall at all?"

"I miss the climate which is always very mild, and the moors." "The moors?" asked Jesse curiously. "Yes, my family's home is just outside Bodmin and my brother and I often go riding in Bodmin moors. It's very beautiful and riding in the mist between the bog and the rough tor is dangerous but exciting at the same time." The description of his home sounded like something out of a Sherlock Holmes murder mystery. Jesse tried to picture his family. His mother sounded like a warm, caring person. "I was rather curious about how you got your tan? Is it from working in the vineyards?" she asked inquiringly. "Some of it I suppose. My mother is actually Italian, so I suppose that's where the tan comes from." They seemed to chat quite easily and both interviewer and interviewee allowed some of their guard down. "How about you, where are you from?" "Well, I spent my childhood in Namibia. My maternal grandmother and my mother raised me. When my gran died, my mother and I moved to South Africa. I remember very little about Namibia though and South Africa is now my home. I have never met my father. Incidentally, he's British," she said casually. Josh detected a slight trace of pain in her voice but he didn't say anything.

The food was delicious and Josh had still not said anything about his behaviour earlier in the day. Jesse decided to bring it up. "You asked me here to talk, to clarify things. I'd like to know what you were referring to." "I wanted to get to know my opponent better," he answered derisively. Jesse lifted her brow in astonishment. "Oh don't pretend to be surprised! You journalists are all the same. After a juicy story." he scoffed. "You're right, Mr Bolton," the familiarity had suddenly left and she realized that the gallant Josh Bolton was replaced by the arrogant landowner, "I am after a good story. But you're wrong about all journalists being the same! I am here to uncover something that will make history in my country. Once this story is published, it will encourage other farmers and workers to see that there is a better way of handling the land crisis in South Africa. But then again you have no loyalty to this country. You are not a citizen. What do you care?" she added mockingly. Jesse fumed with uncontrollable anger. This man had such a nerve implying that she was merely a gossip columnist. What did he think she had studied all those years at the Tech, to learn how to write gossip stories! "Do not pretend to know what I care about Ms Kearns," he again emphasized her title, "and yes, you're right I'm not a citizen but I do care about this country. I love South Africa." "You don't love South Africa!" she raised her voice. "You don't love this country! You love the money that you can make here! You don't care a flying fart about our people! You'll make as much money as you can in the land of milk and honey, leave behind a bunch of half breeds and flee to your beloved England again!" Jesse had to struggle to keep back her tears. "It's happened since time immemorial." People at neighbouring tables started looking in their direction as their voices grew louder and louder. "You English men think that moral codes of behaviour don't apply to you when you're in 'Darkest Africa', you can do what you want, to the uncivilized heathens…" she almost screamed in exasperation. "Please don't blame me if your father didn't marry your mother," he retorted, "that had nothing to do with me or any English man," he replied calmly. His sharp words cut to her heart like a cold knife. She had to catch her breath in order to brace herself for the impact of his words. "How dare you speak about my personal life? Something of which, you clearly know absolutely nothing about." Jesse pushed back her chair and stood up calmly. "I have had more than enough of you for one night. I know the way out Mr Bolton!" she remarked sarcastically. Jesse walked blindly out of the restaurant suddenly aware that people were looking at her and heads were turning as she passed. Once outside, the street was quiet and cool. She gasped for air, filling her lungs in order to calm herself down and refusing to admit to herself that she was frightened. She started walking in the direction of the hotel. The ground was uneven and she had to tread carefully in the dark. Jesse heard strange noises coming from the trees or was it the bushes or the black night sky? Relieved to have left Josh behind she tried to think of nothing else but getting back to her hotel, though, his cold words kept cutting into her heart. Suddenly she was aware of a car pulling up slowly alongside her. Jesse couldn't determine whether she was too frightened or too independent to look at the driver of the car. "C'mon, don't be foolish. Get in the car, I'll take you back to the hotel," Josh commanded. Josh was embarrassed by Jesse's outburst in the restaurant but he found her temper amazingly seductive. She seemed so innocent of his accusations but he could not be certain. Her outburst had proven that she was harbouring many ill feelings toward her biological father and he had certainly unleashed a very painful memory within her. But at this point, he had to keep her from finding out anything about his pending predicament. She did not answer him and continued walking. Suddenly a hand grabbed her arm and spun her around. She looked straight into Josh Bolton's rock hard chest. Again, she smelled his familiar aftershave drowning her senses. She was angry and hurt but tried desperately not to show her pain. She wanted nothing to do with this callous excuse of a man. "Let me go!" she protested trying to dig her heels into the ground. Who was she kidding? Before she could say '*Jack Robinson,*' she lay sprawled across the front seat of the car. "I won't tolerate your childish behaviour," he drawled calmly. Jesse tried to open the passenger door but Josh had already centrally locked the car. She sat cowering in the corner of her seat, looking out into the dark night. But all she could see was her own reflection in the passenger window. There was a deadly silence between them - neither one of them, wanting to be the first to address the issue. Once they had reached the hotel, the car purred to a halt and Josh turned off the engine. Jesse opened the door and nearly bolted up the stairs to the hotel entrance. She did not close the door behind her nor did she turn to say 'good night', although she could feel his eyes furiously blazing through her back.

Once in the safety of her room, she locked her door and breathed a sigh of relief. Jesse realized that her head was actually throbbing by now and she took two headache pills, put her shorty pygamas on and lay down eventually falling into a deep restless sleep where images of her father were haunting her.

Chapter Three

By the time Jesse woke up, she could hear the traffic in the main road. She sat up in bed wondering what time it was when suddenly last nights events came flooding back to her mind. 'Oh Lord, I can't believe that this has actually happened. What on earth possessed me to agree to go out with that chauvinist pig?' Jesse decided to have a long bath, think things through carefully and start the day afresh. She walked into the bathroom and glanced at herself in the mirror. She was shocked to see her red eyes and puffy face, all from last night's crying. She could not allow anyone to see her like this. After she had run her bath and added the much needed salts and bath oil, Jesse got in for a long soak. It felt so good lying in the warm water that she decided to take a deep breath and slip deeper under the water until her entire head was covered. She could not hear any of the noises outside or inside the hotel. There was simply stillness, as if everything had frozen in time. She emerged from the water feeling much better and she knew exactly what she was going to do. She was going to play Josh Bolton at his own game.

As Jesse came out of the bathroom draped in a towel, there was a knock at the door. "Room service," the voice on the other side called. 'I haven't ordered any breakfast yet,' thought Jesse. She opened the door and all she could see was a huge bouquet of flowers. A hotel staff member held out the flowers and said, "This was delivered early this morning for you, m'am." Jesse asked whom it was from but the hotel staff member said that there was no card. Closing the door, she placed the beautiful bouquet on the dresser and realized that the stakes had just been raised. "So this is your game plan Mr Bolton," she said aloud. After breakfast, Jesse took the flowers to a retirement village. "Good morning my dear, how can I help?" asked the elderly woman behind the reception desk. "Good morning, these are for all the lovely ladies. They are from Mr Joshua Bolton of *Sonder Moeite* farm. Please be sure to call him to let him know that you have received the flowers," said Jesse coyly. "Oh my! How thoughtful of him. They're beautiful. I'll call him right away," exclaimed the woman excitedly. Jesse left quickly trying to hide her smile and feeling relieved that for once she had had a say in the matter.

Driving to the library, Jesse decided to do some research on the history of farming in Robertson so that she could have enough background information for her article. As she got out of her car, her mobile phone rang. It was Mitch. "Are you making any headway with the article?" he asked curiously. "Mitch, what possessed you to let me interview this arrogant..." "Now, now Jesse," he cut her short, "may I remind you what cutting edge journalism is all about? It has nothing to do with you and everything to do with getting the information for a good story. I would advise you to swallow your pride and your principles, go, and interview the man. Remember you only have three more working days," he added curtly. "Yes boss!" she saluted the phone before switching it off. Jesse headed for the library to uncover some of the history of this sleepy town. She found many interesting details about Robertson. She read all about how fertile the land was and how successful wine farming had been in the valley for generations. How certain farms were handed down from generation to generation as well as the disputes involving inheritances. Phillip McKinley, the librarian said that the, "*Sonder Moeite* farm was owned for many generations by a Dutch descendent family, the 'van Aards'. But the eldest son was not very interested in farming. When his father died the younger son didn't realize that farming was such hard work." "So what happened?" asked Jesse curiously. "Apparently he ran the farm into the ground by living lavishly on credit. He was forced to sell the farm at a huge loss, that's how Joshua Bolton came into the picture. He bought *Sonder Moeite* for a song."

Jesse spent the better part of the day at the library and only emerged once she felt that she had sufficient information for her article.

Stepping out into the bright sunshine seemed to warm her heart and soften her resolve for revenge. She walked towards her car outside the library. Walking awkwardly with files and paper in one hand while digging into her handbag for her car keys with the other, she looked up and saw Josh leaning casually against her car. The sun shone sneakily, hiding half of his face in its shadow. For a moment, she almost thought she saw him smile. He wore tight jeans, which hugged his long muscular legs. His shirtsleeves were tight, emphasizing his strong tanned muscular biceps. He wore dark mirrored sunglasses showing her reflection in them. His lean frame seemed to be sprawled across the side of her car. He was so darn sexy.

Josh looked at the wisps of her hair that the breeze gently blew about her face. He couldn't help wondering what it was about Jesse Kearns that got under his skin. But if she thought that she could brush him off or his gesture of a truce, she had another thing coming. Josh was as cool as a cucumber. Like a predator on a hunt, he waited for his prey to make the first move. "Please move away from my car!" Jesse ordered in as civil a manner as she could muster. "I'll move away from your car when you tell me why you gave my flowers to a bunch of old women?" he enquired mockingly. "I gave them away because I don't like flowers and I prefer people to apologize in person rather than use a decoy when they have offended me!" she stated passionately. "There isn't a woman on earth who doesn't like flowers. But then again, you are one of a kind, aren't you Ms Kearns?"

"What are you implying?" Jesse asked trying to read between the lines. "Look, perhaps we got off on the wrong foot, maybe we should start the interview all over again," he confessed. 'The wrong foot! What was he talking about,' thought Jesse. He needed a foot in his mouth as far as she was concerned. "There's no need for that Mr Bolton. I have all the information I need in order to write my article.

The town librarian, Phillip McKinley, was a great help. I'll be writing up my article in Cape Town," she revealed, hoping that he would try and persuade her to stay on longer. She had to beat Josh at his own game. "Now if you don't mind, I'd like to get into my car," she feigned impatience. Josh moved towards her in one sweeping movement and pulled her against his hard body. "You're not going back to Cape Town just yet!" he growled. She could feel his breath against her cheek. He looked deep into her eyes and for a moment, she thought she saw something troubled in his expression. He held her in his strong arms pulling her closer to him. His gaze burned into her huge dark eyes and suddenly he lowered his head and his lips found hers. Their mouths melted together. Her lips were full and sweet. Jesse was completely helpless. She couldn't stop herself. She wanted more. Nobody had ever kissed her like that before. Josh tasted her sweetness exploring her mouth with his tongue, desperately wanting to know more about her body. She was tingling all over. Suddenly he stopped and pulled away from her. "Now I know you're not going back to Cape Town yet." "What do you mean?" she stammered, confused. "You have an interview at *Sonder Moeite*," he said walking towards his car. "I'll see you in a short while," he instructed coolly. And with those words, he got into his dark sports car, let the top down and drove off. She could see the glint of his sunglasses reflected in his rearview mirror as he drove away. Jesse pinched herself. 'Aarrhh! He has done it again. He has made a fool of me again and I allowed it! How could I be so stupid? I let down my guard and lost sight of my professionalism.' Josh Bolton had established control of the situation once again by manipulating her senses, her body. Jesse could not believe that he had kissed her. Was he using her or was he genuinely attracted to her? Jesse was confused, she couldn't figure out what had just happened.

Anyway, she wanted the interview and he was willing to give it to her. She needed the information for her article and her boss, Mitch, was depending on her. With that, Jesse drove towards *Sonder Moeite*. The Jacaranda lined driveway met Jesse again and was becoming a pleasantly familiar sight to her. Jesse walked up the steps of the Dutch styled house for the third time. The housekeeper led her into the living room where there was a pot of tea and freshly baked muffins and biscuits waiting for her. Jesse realized that she had not eaten all day and the smell of the freshly baked cake made her suddenly hungry. Josh entered the room and as if he had read her thoughts, he poured her tea and offered her some cake. Once the ceremony of pouring and serving the tea and cake was over, they both ate heartily. Jesse took out her notepad while she sipped her tea. She looked keenly at Josh trying to hide her embarrassment of his earlier kiss. He sat sprawled on the leather sofa opposite her without a care in the world... or so it seemed. His long legs stretched out in front of him. His shirt was unbuttoned halfway down his chest. Jesse could see long black curly hair tumbling about in confusion on his chest. Somehow, he reminded her of James Bond or rather the suave Sean Connery acting as Mr Bond – with his unbuttoned shirt and his seductive seating position. Instinctively, he seemed to know what she was thinking. "Do you like what you see Ms Kearns?" he asked sarcastically. Jesse turned slightly red trying to hide her embarrassment. "Josh, I came here for information on your farm," she said in as business like a manner as she could gather. "My time is running out quickly, so can we get to it, please?" "Alright, I hope you can write fast. I came to South Africa on holiday and did what most tourists do, visited the Robertson wine route. I fell in love with this place instantly and knew that this was where I wanted to live. I knew absolutely nothing about wine farming, so I studied every piece of literature I could get on wine, vines and viticulture." Jesse was in awe of this man. His belief and confidence in himself made her secretly admire him. "*Sonder Moeite* was up for sale, so I purchased it immediately. Initially, I didn't realize what I had inherited from the previous owner. The farm was a bit neglected, but I was determined to pull it together in the shortest possible time. We literally worked day and night to get the farm back in shape for the first harvest of the grapes." Josh spoke with such pride that one couldn't but admire his determination and courage. "What were the major challenges you faced during that first year?" asked Jesse curiously. "Well, I had a lot of challenges with the language, Afrikaans, which most of the workers spoke. I had to contend with their suspicion of foreigners, which I must admit I only understood later when I got to learn more about the history of this country." "So was your idea of worker-shareholders based on those initial challenges?" enquired Jesse. "Oh yes, absolutely. During the first year it seemed as though I was simply crisis managing." He spoke in detail about his struggles on the farm during his initial year. "Then I decided to sort out the problems once and for all and concentrate on production and profit. And I must say things have worked out wonderfully." "Did your background in horse breeding have any influence on this farm?" asked Jesse. "Actually I don't have much of a background in horse breeding. My father and my brother Nico are involved with horses. They have a mutual friend Bill, who helps to train the horses. My background is in property development." "Oh, something like Donald Trump?" she asked deliberately. Josh gave Jesse a quizzical look. "Not on such a grand scale. After completing my MBA at the University of London, I went into business with my former roommate. We bought a small plot of land together and then sold it later at a profit. And that's what I've been doing ever since."

"So you enjoy the property business then?" "It's not so much that I enjoy the property business. It's the wheeling and dealing that attracts me," he added slyly. They spoke for hours without realizing the passing time. Jesse looked at her watch and nearly jumped out of her chair. "Oh no! Look at the time. I have to get back to the hotel. It's already pitch dark outside," she said slightly frightened. Josh immediately saw how tense she had become. "If you think I'm going to allow you to drive to the hotel in the dark, you've got another thing coming," he informed her. Giving instructions came naturally to him. Relieved at his suggestion she remarked, "Thanks, I would really appreciate it if you drove behind me because I really don't know this area at night." "Drive behind you!" he exclaimed. "I don't even drive around here at night; it's too dark to see anything and the winding road back to town can be very dangerous at night! You're sleeping here tonight." "But I…" "No buts, you're sleeping here and that's final," Josh ordered. "I'll get my housekeeper to prepare the guest room for you. His suggestion – or rather his orders seemed practical and intended for her safety. She couldn't argue with him because he knew the area well enough to determine whether it was dangerous for her to travel back to the town. Jesse succumbed once more to the orders of Josh Bolton.

Josh led Jesse to the most charming room she had ever seen. There was a four-poster bed with white organza curtains draped around it. It looked like something out of *The Princess and the Pea* fairytale. It made Jesse almost want to check how many mattresses were on the bed. There was a red rose Cape Dutch porcelain basin mounted in a carved wooden sink frame with a matching porcelain jug for washing. An adjoining room opened into a modernized ensuite bathroom with plush towels and an assortment of bath oils, salts and bubbles. "Please help yourself to anything and shout if there is something that you need." "I'm sure I'll be fine, thanks." As Josh shut the door behind him, Jesse headed for the bathroom. She undressed and had a long warm shower. Feeling more relaxed after her shower she entered the bedroom wrapped in a towel and only then realized that she didn't have any sleepwear with her. To her surprise, draped on the bed was the most beautiful full-length black see through negligee she had ever seen. It was made of the softest black chiffon. The bodice was made of black Chantilly lace and the breast cups had a thin row of black sequence bordering them. "Is this for me?" Jesse asked herself looking around as though there were someone to answer her question. She slipped the negligee on and gazed at herself in the mirror. Suddenly she saw Josh in her

28

reflection. Embarrassed she covered her chest feeling terribly exposed. Josh gazed at her intently. He longed for her but she was wearing another woman's nightdress. "Goodnight, sleep well." He turned and left the room abruptly shutting the door. Jesse stared at the shut bedroom door. 'Was he so repulsed by me that he couldn't stand to look at me?' Josh had a way of making her feel rejected without even saying anything unkind. She gazed at herself in the full-length mirror next to the washstand. She didn't think that she looked too bad. Jesse wondered whose negligee she was wearing. The owner was definitely taller than she was because the bottom of the negligee was touching the floor and the spaghetti straps kept falling off her narrow shoulders. But Jesse had to admit that the owner of this garment really had style and exquisite taste.

Lying in bed Jesse reflected on the days events. Josh Bolton had kissed her. She giggled like a teenager again. He was so difficult to figure out. Most of the time he seemed nice and then that awful arrogance would creep in and spoil everything. She wondered what kind of women he had dated. If they were anything like the negligee she was wearing then they had to be very wealthy and powerful women. Maybe that's why he treated her with consideration and scorn at the same time. She didn't have the kind of money and power that he was used to. She had to be very careful of this man. She lay there amongst the one hundred percent percale sheets and reflected on the days events. She had to be careful of Joshua Bolton. Men like Joshua Bolton were only after one thing. But he had kissed her,' giggled Jesse. Jesse fell sound asleep with a wicked smile on her beautiful face. That night she dreamt she was walking in a field of yellow and white daisies and every time she picked a white daisy, a little girl replaced the daisy. The little girl looked just like her but she had Josh's dimple on her cheek. When she picked a yellow daisy, a laughing little boy with Josh's mocking eyes replaced the yellow daisy.

When Jesse opened her eyes the next day, the sun was streaming through the window. She was disoriented for a moment and then suddenly realized where she was. There was a cup of cold coffee on the nightstand and a note. She opened the note to read, *'How about a picnic luncheon for two at the farm river?'* Josh's name was added to the bottom of the note. His handwriting was long, curvy and bold. The note seemed to have been written by someone who was extremely influential. Jesse looked at her watch and noticed that it was almost ten o'clock. She scrambled into her clothes and somehow managed to straighten her tousled hair. The housekeeper met Jesse in the passage on her way out. "Good morning, I overslept," she stammered apologetically. "It must be the country air," responded the housekeeper. Jesse couldn't make out if she was being nice or sarcastic. "Do you know where the farm river is?"

"Yes, before you reach the gate on your way out just turn right and that road will take you to the river," answered the housekeeper. Jesse thanked her and headed back to her hotel for a quick shower and a change of clothes.

Her heart was racing as she got out of the shower. Jesse wondered why she was becoming so intrigued by such a brusque man. Was it his inexplicable attitude that she was drawn to or was it some peculiar interest she had in his past? She could not forget the negligee and was determined to ask him about it. She slipped on some khaki pants and a loose white cotton shirt with flat tan sandals.

It was a beautiful sunny Thursday morning when she drove out to the river on the *Sonder Moeite* farm. Jesse didn't know what to expect. She saw Josh's 4x4 vehicle and parked her car next to his. She had to walk about twenty-five paces to where he was standing. He stood on a large rock throwing pebbles into the river. They hopped as they bounced off the water. She watched him as he tried to make the pebbles hop more than three times on the water. He seemed incredibly athletic.

Josh turned as she approached and walked towards her. She noticed that he looked very relaxed and rested. "Hello sleepy head, I hope you're hungry?" he teased. Trying to hide her embarrassment, she feebly defended herself, "I was tired. Have you any idea how tiring it is interviewing you?" Before he could respond she retorted, "And yes, I am starving." He pointed to a blanket under a tree and said, "Well, I've catered for your needs or at least my housekeeper has." "Thank you Josh, that was very kind of both of you. I can assure you I won't disappoint you. I could eat a horse." Josh wondered where all the food would fit into Jesse's tiny frame.

The picnic basket contained rye bread with marmalade, crackers with cottage cheese, banana bread, yogurt, fresh fruit juice and a fruit salad. Everything looked fresh and delicious and Jesse didn't know where to start. It reminded her of her own life. There were so many options, choices and decisions to make that she was afraid of making the wrong choice and missing out on the best things. Josh noticed her confusion and decided to choose for her. "You have to try Beth's rye bread; it's the best bread I've ever eaten." She was grateful that he had chosen the bread for her and noticed that he had an uncanny way of reading her thoughts. They ate in silence for a while looking past the river and over the valley from the hill they were sitting on. The Langeberg Mountains seemed mysterious yet gloomy as they brazenly protected the valley. The view was truly spectacular.

The air was crisp and fresh and everything seemed quiet and peaceful. The sun shone warmly on the rows and rows of vines that stretched into the distance on the other side of the river. The blue hills in the distance, forming part of the Langeberg mountain range, seemed to also envelop the *Sonder Moeite* vineyards and the river in an effort to protect this precious land from intruders. "You have really made a good choice," said Jesse staring into the distance. "The bread?" Josh asked puzzled. "No, *Sonder Moeite*. It's such a beautiful piece of land," said Jesse dreamily. "I agree, I wish I could share this with someone," he answered unguarded. She looked at him, surprised, and noticed that troubled look in his eyes once again. Seizing the moment, she asked, "Josh, who does the black negligee I wore last night belong to?" He paused and then answered, "To be very honest, I have no idea. I left England in a terrible hurry. All I remember is that there was a lot of un-ironed washing on my bed, which I bundled into my suitcase and came here. My housekeeper, Beth, found it and hung it in the guestroom closet." Jesse looked at him suspiciously and wanted to ask what a negligee was doing in his un-ironed washing but his expression changed her mind. Josh suddenly looked tired, as if he had the weight of the world on his shoulders.

There was so much that he wanted to tell her - but the moment was not right. She wanted to ask him about his personal life but felt that she was intruding on forbidden territory. Suddenly his mobile phone rang. "Yes, Jaco," he queried. "The electricity has been cut again, boss. We need to use a generator to grind the grapes in the tanks before they start to ferment," answered Jaco. "We don't have a generator?" asked Josh. "No boss, you have to buy one in town, now!" Josh detected the urgency in Jaco's voice. "I'll be there as soon as I can!" he said switching off his phone. "Trouble?" asked Jesse. "Yes, I'm sorry. You'll have to finish the picnic on your own if you don't mind. If I don't move now I might lose a big portion of my harvest. I'll call you later," he said getting into his vehicle. Jesse watched the dust lift into the air as he drove away.

Chapter Four

Jesse did not hear from Josh all day or the next. She realized that he must have still been in a crisis situation - trying to salvage his harvest. There was no more point in her hanging around as she had obtained all the necessary information for her article. Jesse decided to check out of her hotel and head back to Cape Town.

She arrived just after lunch and the task of writing her article was now her main priority. Josh did not attempt to contact her that weekend and Jesse decided that Robertson was merely an interesting chapter in her life. But try as she may, she couldn't stop thinking about him.

Early on Tuesday morning Jesse sat glued to her laptop computer at the office. She was adding the final changes to her article and by lunchtime, she handed her article to Mitch hoping that he would be happy with it. Jesse hated comebacks. Anyway, she was tired of writing and decided to go and sit in a coffee shop. She ordered a sandwich with herbal tea and later decided to indulge herself with a pancake and ice cream. When she got back to the office there was an envelope on her desk. The handwriting looked hauntingly familiar. She was shaking with anticipation as she opened the envelope. There was a card inside. Opening it carefully, she read it slowly to herself. *'Dear Jesse,'* it read, *'You left without saying goodbye. Robertson will be celebrating its annual wine festival starting this Friday. I am inviting you to stay at Sonder Moeite for the weekend. It will be very interesting and you may learn a lot for your articles. Please let me know soon, so I can send someone to fetch you. Josh.'*

Jesse could not believe this. She was very surprised. She read the invitation repeatedly, trying to read between the lines. The first sentence sounded a bit sad or was it disappointment she read. Then he invited her to stay at *Sonder Moeite*. Was there a motive behind his invitation? What were his intentions? Did he mean it would be interesting in general? Did he mean it would be interesting between them? What was she to make of this? It drove her crazy. Who would he send to fetch her?

Mitch walked in with a smile on his face. "I knew I could count on you," he beamed. "Very good work, Jesse!" Mitch had a way of always making her feel appreciated. "Did you know that Robertson has an annual wine festival?" she inquired. "In fact I heard it being advertised on the radio last week. Why?"

"Josh Bolton invited me to spend the weekend and participate in the festivities," she said shyly. "Hmm, do I smell romance in the air?" Mitch asked curiously. "We'll see," Jesse answered vaguely, trying to camouflage her feelings. "I'm putting in a day's leave on Friday. I'd like to see what this wine weekend is all about."

"Just be careful, Jesse. Remember to look after yourself." Mitch was always looking out for her and it made her feel special when he worried about her.

So it was settled then. She called Josh but his mobile phone was switched off so she left a message that she'd love to come and experience the wine festival. Early on Friday morning Josh's driver picked up Jesse at her flat. She had collected a few brochures from the tourism office in Cape Town on the Robertson wine route and decided to read more about the history of wine in the area in order to educate herself before she got there.

They drove straight to *Sonder Moeite* where the housekeeper, Beth, met Jesse on the front steps. "Mr Bolton is in town helping with the organizing of the wine weekend. Let me show you to your room," she chirped politely. Even Beth seemed excited about the wine weekend. "What happens in Robertson during the wine festival?"

asked Jesse naively. "We have live bands playing in the town square; there are stalls where you can buy freshly made traditional food. There is even a jam preserve competition for the best homemade jam. Then there is the wine auction and tours on the different wine estates where you can observe the wine making process," added Beth gleefully. "Well, I hope you are entering your marmalade jam in the competition," encouraged Jesse laughingly. "I am, I am," laughed Beth. 'I'm really looking forward to this weekend,' she thought to herself.

Josh arrived at the house about a half hour later. Jesse had just finished unpacking her suitcase when she suddenly looked up and saw him. His frame filled the doorway and she detected his very mischievous dimple, which momentarily flashed across his cheek. "How long have you been standing there," she asked guardedly. Josh ignored her question. "Good morning Ms Kearns. Are you ready to leave?" She never knew where she stood with him. One minute he was all concerned and caring and the next, he was an aloof arrogant businessman. "Good morning and yes I am ready to leave and I had a good trip as well, just in case you wanted to know," she added sarcastically. "Glad to hear that," he played along pretending not to notice her bite.

They drove to the town square with Beth chattering away excitedly about who could be a possible winner in the jam preserve competition. She did not forget to bring a box of jars filled with her famous marmalade jam. When they arrived, there was a lot of activity. People were setting up stalls to sell their goods. Others were already selling their displayed items and the sound engineer was testing the equipment on the large stage. "One, two, one, two," his voice boomed out of the speakers. There was a lot of excitement in the air. "You will have to excuse me," indicated Josh. "I have to ensure that the sound for the auction is properly set up." "Of course," nodded Jesse. He disappeared into a small crowd of people and Jesse turned to help Beth unpack her jam jars.

Beth had already filled in the forms for the competition and the judges had received all the jam from the various participants. Jesse decided to wonder around to see what everybody else was selling. She walked from stall to stall, stopping now and then to chat to a stall owner and ask some questions. She bought some homemade chocolate and cake and nibbled away while she was admiring the crafts on display. Suddenly she heard her name being called across the crowd. She couldn't see who was calling her. Then she saw him wave at her. It was Phillip McKinley, the town librarian. How nice of him to remember her, she thought. Jesse waved back and he strolled shyly over toward her.

"Jesse, hello," he stammered. "How nice of you to come to our annual wine festival!" he exclaimed. "Hello, Phillip. I'm glad I came. I wouldn't have missed it for the world." "Come let me show you around." He was very keen to show Jesse all the interesting things on display. Phillip launched into a history of how the annual wine festival started and how the auction really worked. "You see, when a farmers wine is being auctioned and it fetches a very high price, people automatically think that it must be a good wine. It gives that particular wine label a lot of publicity locally and internationally. It also means that tourists want to visit the wine estate and that also brings in a lot of revenue," he added excitedly. "So whose wine fetched the highest price last year?" asked Jesse curiously. "It was the Meiring wine farm. They produce the best chardonnay. But competition is very stiff this year. I hear Joshua Bolton is trying for first prize this year." Jesse looked very surprised. "He is?" she asked curiously. Just then, Jesse felt a firm hand grip her arm. She shot around but before she could say anything, "Excuse us Phil," growled Josh. Phil turned red, not knowing what to say. Josh steered her expertly away. "What in the name of ..." she uttered. Josh's clenched jaw was pulsating. "You didn't come here to spend time with Phil," he ordered. "How could you be so rude to him?" Jesse asked embarrassed. "I've been looking all over for you and never mind Phil!" he growled.

"We need a journalist to cover the auction." She wasn't sure if he was asking her or telling her. "What?" responded Jesse, shocked? "The journalist who was supposed to cover the story couldn't make it on the last minute. Do you want the story?" he asked temptingly. "Yes, of course," Jesse shrieked jumping into Josh's arms. It was like a dream come true. Only a journalist could understand the excitement of such an opportunity. Josh held her for a second longer in his arms. His eyes burned into hers as if he were searching for something. Again, she noticed that troubled look in his eyes. "What is it, Josh?" she asked worried. "Stay away from Phillip McKinley!" he ordered. "I beg your pardon?" retorted Jesse. "I mean it!" Before she could respond, he walked away towards the stage. What in the world was that all about? Was Josh trying to warn her about Phillip or was he just jealous? Anyway, Jesse didn't have time to contemplate Josh's behaviour. The man was truly an enigma.

Jesse was glad that she usually traveled prepared. In her bag, she had a notepad, a micro recorder and a hand digital camcorder. Mitch would be very impressed with another story on Robertson. She thought that she would give it a different angle this time. Maybe a tourism or economic angle would be of interest to readers she thought. Jesse headed toward the stage so she could get a front row seat. Most of the front seats had already been taken and some were reserved for VIP's. "Excuse me m'am, are you the journalist?" asked an official. "Yes," responded Jesse surprised. "This way please" he indicated for her to follow him and led her to a seat in the middle of the front row, so she had a clear view. She saw her name printed on a page in bold letters pinned on the back of the seat. JOURNALIST: JESSE KEARNS. She was so surprised. Josh had acted very quickly.

His plan seemed to have been contrived. Did Josh invite her here knowing that she would do this story? This seemed odd. He didn't seem as though he had a motive to get her to the wine festival. She dismissed the thought immediately and decided to enjoy the proceedings.

Someone on the stage rang a bell and the crowd settled down. Josh took the microphone in his hand and greeted the crowd. There was loud cheering and some women even shouted admiring remarks. Jesse could see why everyone was so taken with this Englishman. Josh's athletic looks were undeniably striking. But his voice was the coup de grace. It was deep and intimate expressing each syllable individually. It was as if he was whispering to Jesse alone. She was sure that most of the women felt that he was talking to them alone too. She began to reminisce about his kiss and started becoming moist at the thought of him so close to her. Then she heard Josh say something about his journalist friend and he looked towards her and winked. Jesse felt tormented by him. Was he playing the fool with her or was he being serious? She heard him mention a farm's name and describe the wine produced there. He made jokes in between or gave some interesting information about the farm or the farm owner. He spoke in detail about chardonnay, Pinotage and Shiraz wines. Jesse couldn't keep up with the information. She put her pen down and started recording Josh. He hit the gavel every time he made a sale. "Going once, going twice, sold…" He seemed to know exactly how to wow the crowd. Then it was time for the *Sonder Moeite* wine to be auctioned. Jesse saw Josh step aside to an official and speak to him privately. The official took the microphone and addressed the crowd. He said that Mr Bolton did not feel comfortable auctioning his own wine so he had asked the official to do so. The crowd roared with disapproval. People were shouting from the back for Bolton to come back. Eventually the crowd shouted in unison. "Bolton, Bolton, Bolton…" Jesse had to smile; she had no idea that Josh commanded so much respect in the town. Eventually Josh took the microphone and proceeded with the auction of the *Sonder Moeite* wine. He began with the *Sonder Moeite* Merlot and proceeded to explain the body and the taste of the wine. Jesse videoed him on stage and then turned the camera to the crowd. The crowd was shouting as the price seemed to go higher and higher. They all wanted to be the highest bidder of the *Sonder Moeite* wine. Coincidentally, most of the bidders for the *Sonder Moeite* wine were women. A woman sitting next to Jesse whispered to her, "The *Sonder Moeite* wine is the best in the Robertson valley." Jesse nodded in approval, unable to let the woman know that she didn't have a clue about wine. Jesse also got the impression that the women were vying for Josh's attention. She couldn't blame them. This wine festival was becoming very serious business and she was determined to learn more.

Josh, the auctioneer of the day, eventually auctioned off the last bottle of wine and the last barrel of wine for that particular day. Everybody started moving off toward the food stalls and the dust seemed to settle as the crowd edged slowly away. Jesse packed her equipment away and waited for Josh to finish. He walked slowly down the steps towards her looking weary from all the excitement. "Congratulations!" she squealed excitedly. "Thank you and thanks for being here." He looked at her as if he wanted to say something else, then he changed his mind and said, "We ought to be heading home. It's been a long day. Let's go and fetch Beth." Josh took hold of her elbow and escorted Jesse to Beth's food stall. By the time they reached Beth, she had already packed up her stall. "So, what happened?" asked Josh. "I won second prize for my jam, Mrs Cornelius came first with her fig jam," said Beth excitedly. "Well, we are certainly taking honours back to *Sonder Moeite,*" said Josh proudly.

They were all tired by the time they got home and everybody departed quietly to their own quarters. Jesse had a long refreshing shower and changed into a short shift dress. By the time she came back to the living room, Beth had set a side table with sandwiches, tea and some cake. She bent over and poured herself some tea. "Make that two," requested Josh. Jesse looked up to see Josh staring at her legs. His eyes ravished her body. Her cheeks turned red, she didn't know where to look. She handed him a cup and his fingers brushed ever so slightly against hers. Jesse could feel her thighs warming and her heart begin to race. Why was her body betraying her? She wasn't even sure if she liked Josh Bolton. They had tea and ate together until she excused herself and said good night.

Chapter Five

Jesse undressed and changed into her short pink satin negligee with lace edging. She lay on her side stretched out on the bed looking at the video clipping she had taken earlier of the auction. There was a soft knock at her door. 'It must be Beth coming to inquire if I'm comfortable,' she thought. "Come in Beth," Jesse called. The door opened, as she turned around to look at Beth. Instead, Josh stood in the doorway. He stood with half his body in the shadow of the passage light. Jesse could not see his face properly nor read his intentions. Josh stood languidly without saying anything, taking in her long bronze well-toned legs. He stood for a moment without saying anything. Jesse was embarrassed and tried to pull her negligee further down her knees in an attempt at modesty but there just wasn't sufficient fabric.

Gathering her courage together and hoping that she did not betray herself again she asked, "Is there something you wanted?" Josh took what seemed like a giant step and he was at the bed. He scooped her up in his arms and buried his head in her neck. Jesse was shocked at his intense display of lust but she did not protest. She had very similar thoughts that she had tried in vain to extinguish. His lips found the soft curve of her neck as he kissed her wantonly and she made soft moaning noises as he kissed her neck and caressed her ear with his tongue.

Jesse tried to gather what was left of her senses, "Josh no! What are you doing?" "Don't pretend as if you don't want this. Ever since I kissed you at the library, you've wanted more." "That's a lie," she protested feebly. "Don't worry, I can't stop thinking about you either," he uttered frantically. He searched automatically for her breasts, cupping them in his strong hard hands. Her nipples responded by perking up in anticipation. Her swollen breasts filled his roving hands and his mouth found her tender swell. He kissed her

41

breasts burying his head in her valley. Jesse moaned his name under her breath, "Oh, Joshua, don't stop." His mouth found hers and her warm sweet lips responded with just as much urgency. He wanted all of her. He couldn't stop himself. It had been so long since he was with a woman. And Jesse was definitely worth the wait.

Pulling her on top of him he gently maneuvered her pink negligee over her shoulders. She was like a bronze goddess, tan and lithe with soft long curly flowing hair, ripe for the plucking. Josh knew he wanted to make love to her instantly. Jesse fumbled with his shirt buttons. "Just tear it off baby," he panted. She ripped his shirt off and found his hard tan chest with black curly hair. He was a sight for sore eyes. Her fingers brushed through his hairy chest searching for his nipples. She caressed him with the tip of her tongue. He sighed with deep satisfaction. Josh put his hand around Jesse's waist, and in one sweeping movement, she was lying underneath him. He looked deep into her eyes as though he was searching for something and once again, she noticed that troubled look in his hazel eyes. His hard legs pressed against her thighs and with shock, she felt his manhood searching for her mound. Jesse had no idea how he removed his pants. He had done it so quickly and expertly like a seasoned lover that she began to feel slightly inadequate. She felt so exposed while he ravished her body. He noticed her tenseness and stopped, lifting his head to gaze at her. Jesse blushed feeling so insecure; she automatically slid her arms over her breasts covering them. "Josh, stop please?" she begged. "Why?"

"I'm not very good at this," she pleaded. "Don't worry. Let me handle this," he added soothingly. "You have beautiful breasts, don't cover them. All you need to do is enjoy the experience." He traced the outline of her body, his hand moving in waves along the curves of her frame. Finally, he was at her inner thigh and moved expertly to her femininity. He caressed her and she tensed with shocked pleasure. Jesse was clearly not used to being seduced by a real man, he thought. Josh lowered himself to her belly and caressed her with his tongue sending sensations so intense that she cried out in delight. His tongue traced her inner thigh until he reached her femininity once again. He flicked his tongue expertly over her soft parts, which made her dizzy with pleasure. Again, she squirmed making a feeble attempt to gain control of her senses but he merely ignored her using his finger to rub her back and forth. It felt so good, which made her feel so bad. Jesse had always, been taught that good girls didn't enjoy such things. Good girls were respectable.

By now, she was weak with pleasure, Josh simply parted her thighs, and his fingers were deep inside her. All sense of reason had long gone out the window. Her body exploded with one intense sensation of pleasure after another. Jesse had no idea that she could feel such emotion. Her breathing was shallow until his mouth found hers again. He kissed her with such passion that her pelvis throbbed with unbearable sexual pleasure. Her senses were begging him to stop but her body betrayed her by pleading for more. He kissed her until she pulled away gasping for air.

He used his powerful leg to thrust her thighs open. She tried in vain to stop the aching sensation in her lower body but his shaft was already searching for her open femininity. He thrust himself gently inside her and her moistness seemed to swallow him in. Josh put his hand under Jesse's waist lifting her up so she could take all of him in. She arched her body inviting him to take her. He pumped her sending off small explosions in her body. She was breathless while his mouth found hers, kissing her sweet soft lips. He continued his unyielding assault on her senses until her body reached its peak and exploded in a fit of ecstasy. Her brain had experienced a pyromaniac's ultimate fantasy and all that remained were the shimmering stars falling from the sky. She clung to him desperately and buried her head in his strong shoulder until the last stars had exploded and fell, landing her back to reality.

Jesse felt embarrassed by her explicit show of passion. She grabbed the sheet when Josh rolled off her and covered herself. "Don't be shy," he said gently. "You were wonderful and your body, it's perfect," he added softly encouraging her. Josh threw the sheet off her and scooped her up in his arms. He carried her into the adjoining bathroom and turned on the shower taps.

Warm water ejaculated out like a welcoming fountain cooling them down. Jesse was grateful for the change of surroundings. Now she could establish some control of herself. Or so she thought. He turned her around in the shower and caressed her back and shoulders. Then he lathered her back stroking the slippery soapsuds over her smooth bronze skin. He embraced her from behind and cupped her breasts. He stroked her and turned her gently to face him. Josh knelt down with the water pelting on him and lifted his head toward her breasts. She was aching for him. She placed her breast in his warm mouth and he kissed her and stroked her nipple with his tongue, sending shivers down her spine. He lifted her right leg over his shoulder and gently flicked his tongue over the soft nub of her femininity. Jesse thought that she would die from the explosion of pleasure. She waited for her body to surrender from the sensations of extreme sexual pleasure but there was more gratification to come. Her head flung back with beads of water cascading down her soft bosom onto his head between her legs. Her body arched intensely as he placed his fingers deep inside her again rubbing her back and forth. She wriggled with wanton pleasure.

Jesse thought that he would never stop then suddenly he turned her around and kissed her, parting her lips and exploring her syrupy mouth with his tongue. Josh rubbed soap all over her again while she slithered in his arms. This time he turned her around and she felt his powerful erection press against her buttocks. He guided his shaft until he found her moist soft feminine part. With a slight thrust, he

44

was deep inside her again. She gave a cry of sheer delight as he thrust in and out of her. All she could hear was his muffled breathing and the gushing water pelting down on them. She wished he would never stop. Eventually she cried out as her body reached a crescendo of passion exploding into a million sensations of extreme erotic pleasure. He moaned softly too and she knew that he had also reached the same peak of passion. Both of them were spent - exhausted with passion and pleasure. He turned her around again and kissed her deep and long as though he was branding her with his final taste. Then he turned off the taps, wrapped a towel around her and carried her back to the bed.

Jesse watched him as he put his clothes on and said goodnight. She looked very surprised when he asked, "Did you think I was going to spend the night?" She opened her mouth to say something but couldn't think of what to say. "The sex was great, thank you," he winked wickedly at her, showing off that unmistakable dimple on his cheek and then left the room closing the door softly behind him. She stared at the closed door in disbelief. How could he be so unfeeling, so callus? She had opened herself up to him.

Jesse sobbed uncontrollably. She sobbed because she had allowed Joshua Bolton to come so close to her heart. She allowed him to explore her body intimately with her. He had just used her. He had thanked her for sex as if she were a sex worker. This was all her fault. 'This is the price you pay for stupidity Jesse Kearns,' she said to herself. She cried herself to sleep once again. That night she dreamed that she was walking in the vineyard picking grapes but when she looked down at herself, her clothes were in rags.

Josh stood outside her bedroom door listening to her quiet sobs. He felt as though he were dying inside. He wanted so much to tell her the truth. He wanted to make her pain go away. He wanted to protect her and scoop her up in his arms. But he had to be careful. He couldn't allow himself to get so close to her, not until he had sorted out his dilemma with Ava. He felt as though there were a noose hanging over his head. But he assured himself that everything would be over in a few short weeks.

Josh could not sleep. He couldn't get Jesse out of his mind. He could still taste her soft sweet lips. He never dreamed a woman could turn him on in this way, not after the way Ava had treated him. He had promised himself that he would never become emotionally involved with a woman again. He had seen how women can manipulate and extricate every ounce of a man with their vicious pursuit of power. The sex with Jesse was astonishingly great and he admitted he hadn't thought it would be. He didn't realize that he had been so starved of the affections of a woman. However, he did not want her to misinterpret his motives. If he allowed her to think that he wanted to get involved with her, it would mean commitments, contracts, and family bondage. He didn't trust any woman enough to want to walk down that road again. Eventually he fell asleep feeling like a man again.

Chapter Six

Jesse was too ashamed to come out of her room the following morning. She dawdled and changed clothes half a dozen times. Eventually she decided on a white wrap around dress with a broad red high waisted belt. She dunked her face in a basin of ice-cold water in the bathroom in an attempt to shrink her puffy eyes from the previous nights crying.

Eventually hunger got the better of her. She came down to the dining area for breakfast. There was nobody in the dining room but the table was set for one. Breakfast was on a side table and Jesse opened dishes of scrambled eggs, sausages and bacon on the warmer. She simply ate a bowl of fruit with muesli and yogurt trying not to think about the previous night's events. How could she have gotten herself into this situation? Everybody knew Jesse Kearns to be a levelheaded young woman. She was just about to finish when Beth came into the room. "Good morning Ms Kearns. Did you sleep well?" asked Beth cheerfully. Jesse smiled faintly and nodded. "Mr Bolton said to tell you that he'd fetch you at eleven o'clock. So he should be here shortly." "Thanks Beth," smiled Jesse trying hard to sound cheerful.

She went up to her room after breakfast, applied some makeup and sat on the bed with her hands under her thighs swinging her legs back and forth, not knowing what to do next. Soon enough she heard Josh's 4x4 vehicle coming up the long driveway. Her fate was sealed in the roar of the vehicle's engine. This time she couldn't run away. Where would she go? 'Oh dear! How am I going to face him? What am I going to say to him?' she panicked. She heard him run up the stairs towards her room and then pound on the door. It was so contrary to his soft knock last night on her bedroom door. "Come in," she called out. "Hello, are you ready?" he asked cheerily. Jesse decided to play it by ear and just go with the flow. If he did not say anything about last night, neither would she. "Yes, let's go." She got up, grabbed her bag and walked out in front of him. She could feel his eyes on her and his step slowed down a fraction. She knew he was scrutinizing her from behind and she turned red with embarrassment. All she had to do now was trip and fall. That would certainly be the cherry on top of her embarrassment. Jesse turned around suddenly and Josh nearly bumped into her. "Stop staring at my butt!" she ordered angrily. "Why? It's a free country. I can admire the view whenever I please," he teased her. Jesse did not know how she was going to face him all day at the festival.

Before long they were in his 4x4 vehicle headed for the wine show. Jesse promised herself that today she would show more professionalism than she had done before. As soon as Josh had parked the vehicle, he opened the passenger door for Jesse.

She lowered herself out of the high vehicle and her wrap dress opened revealing her tan thigh. Josh could not help noticing her attractive lean thighs and once again felt a stirring in his loins. They walked towards the wine auction stage and Jesse saw Phillip McKinley walking towards her. He waved at her and she waved back. Josh grabbed her wrist and held it tightly. "What do you think you're doing?

You're hurting me!" she shrieked at him. "I warned you about that man!" he growled ferociously. "You don't own me," she shot back. "I can speak to whom ever I want." As Phillip approached her, he seemed surprised that Josh was holding her wrist. "Hello Josh," greeted Phillip. "Not now Phil," objected Josh, brushing Phillip aside. "Jesse has to prepare for her interviews," he commanded walking away with her. "I'll chat to you later Phillip," Jesse called out over her shoulder. Poor Phil stood there like a fool, wondering what he had done wrong this time. "Was that necessary?" she asked indignantly. "Was what necessary, my love?"

48

"You were unforgivably rude, Joshua. And since when am I your love?" she demanded. "Since last night, I think," he responded sarcastically. Josh looked at her mockingly, a whimsical smile balancing itself precariously at the corner of his mouth. Jesse blushed and looked the other way. "And by the way, I like it when you call me Joshua," he added slyly. "It is your name, isn't it?" she responded rhetorically. He knew she was trying to be smart. They reached the front row of reserved seats just like the day before. "I'll see you later." He turned and walked up the steps to the stage before she could answer. Jesse stared after him - something seemed different about him. His presence seemed a lot lighter – less strained. Perhaps it was her influence in the bedroom last night. Half embarrassed and half-proud, she smiled secretly to herself.

Jesse watched with deep interest as bidders vied for the best wines. It seemed as if it was also a matter of prestige and honour if one could afford to bid for the more expensive wines. Jesse decided to interview Mrs Vermaak, one of the richest farmers in the valley. She had just bidden on a vintage chardonnay wine and looked very pleased with her successful purchase. Jesse approached her with camera in hand. Mrs Vermaak was a big regal looking woman, possibly in her late fifties with plenty of makeup on and expensive jewelry that really looked quite tacky on her. Someone should definitely have told her that *'less was actually more',* thought Jesse. Jesse approached her with her hand extended, Hello Mrs Vermaak, I'm Jesse Kearns, from the Cape Town Post. I believe you've just claimed some of the finest wine at the auction." "And *r*ightly so, my dea*r*," she rejoined. "The Ve*r*maak family has a fine eye fo*r* quality wines. My late husband was one of the most expe*r*ienced fa*r*me*r*s in the valley," she added emphasizing her r's as she pressed them out with her heavy Afrikaner accent. She went on a tirade of information about her family's history and their well standing position in the wine community. Jesse listened with interest, which gave Mrs Vermaak a wide opening to prattle on about how important and dignified her family members were. "You should *really* come to take some photos of my family and ou*r* estate. Why not come fo*r* tea this afte*r*noon?" she asked expectantly. Jesse did not have the heart to refuse her and ruin her imperial moment of glory. "But I didn't bring my car," Jesse feigned slight disappointment. She thought that this excuse would get her off the hook. But alas! "Don't wo*rr*y my dea*r*; you will come with me once the festivities a*r*e over. Jesse had no choice but to obey. "Okay". "Good, then its settled. We'll have tea this afte*r*noon and I'll tell you all about my sons Jan-Hend*r*ik and Jacobus," she beamed with pride.

Jesse wondered what she had gotten herself into - she hoped that Mrs Vermaak would not be able to find her later in the throngs of people. Now she would have to explain to Josh where she was going. She didn't want to have to report her movements to him though. Still, she wasn't sure if he would like this idea and she was his guest after all. Yet, he was so cold and unfeeling towards her last night and so rude to Phillip today that she decided a little rudeness would be a taste of his own medicine. Jesse interviewed two other people then wondered around the food stalls tasting and buying delicious delicacies. She could hear Josh's voice over the microphone and every time she heard wild applause, she knew he had made a big sale.

Soon she heard someone calling her name. "Jesse, coo wee," it was Mrs Vermaak waddling towards her with large swollen feet bursting out of her expensive pink shoes. "I've been looking all ove*r* fo*r* you child, come it's time to go," she ordered. Mrs Vermaak didn't give Jesse a chance to protest, she grabbed her hand and Jesse had no choice but to obey. "I have to let Josh Bolton know where I'm going, he'll be looking for me," she implored. "Why does he need to know whe*r*e you a*r*e going?" asked Mrs Vermaak lifting a critical eyebrow. Jesse felt suddenly judged and turned red. "Oh Mrs Vermaak, I'm his guest for the weekend at *Sonder Moeite*. "Oh," she sounded relieved, "don't wo*rr*y we'll call him from *Geluks Gedacht*. Jesse seemed puzzled. "That's the name of my estate," laughed Mrs Vermaak. "Isn't it a wonderful name? It means happy thoughts." "Yes, very charming," agreed Jesse. They sat in the back seat of Mrs Vermaak's big expensive American car while one of her workers acted as chauffeur. The ride to *Geluks Gedacht* went by very quickly because Jesse had to listen to Mrs Vermaak prattle on about her late husband, children and grandchildren. By the time they got to the farm, she had enough information to write an article. She wondered which angle she should write from this time.

Mrs Vermaak entered her home with so much aplomb; she had the house help bustling about taking her hat, white gloves and handbag while she issued instructions for tea to be served in her library. Jesse was in awe of her home. It was much bigger than the farmhouse at *Sonder Moeite* and far more stylish. Jesse couldn't believe her eyes when she entered the library. It looked like one of those rooms in Jane Austin's *Pride and Prejudice*. She wondered if Phillip McKinley had been inside this library. There were books from floor to ceiling. Some were very old books bound in leather. Mrs Vermaak noticed Jesse admiring the books and said, "My late husband was an avid book collector and do you know that he actually read most of these books." Mrs Vermaak beamed from ear to ear. Jesse could tell that she was very proud of her late husband. She wished that one day she too could meet a man that would make her so proud.

Tea was served before long and Jesse hungrily dug into her scones, licking the cream and jam off her fingers. Mrs Vermaak poured the tea herself from a rose patterned porcelain teapot. It seemed as if Mrs Vermaak wanted Jesse to write a biography on her family. She brought out old photographs of her family's predecessors and their relatives. "Ooh! You have a gold mine here Mrs Vermaak," exclaimed Jesse. "I know, isn't it wonderful my dear." She informed Jesse about whose marriages had been arranged. Who had inherited from whom? She spoke of family members that had fought over inheritances and were still not on speaking terms decades later. She also told Jesse about men who had married farmer's daughters and squandered all their money and their farms away. But most of all she boasted about her late husband's success as a farmer and how he had taught their sons to be farmers. In her eyes, there would never be another man like the late Mr Vermaak.

Mrs Vermaak spoke so much that Jesse completely forgot about Josh. She insisted that Jesse stay to meet her sons when they came from the vineyards. Time seemed to pass by so quickly while Mrs Vermaak prattled on about *Robertson* and the people in her community. Then she suddenly asked Jesse, "So how do you know Joshua Bolton?" She caught Jesse completely off guard. "Umm, I interviewed him a couple of weeks ago regarding the land redistribution question in South Africa and he invited me back for the wine festival," she added guiltily.

"I don't trust that man. He claims to be an Englishman but have you ever seen such a dark Englishman?" Mrs Vermaak asked skeptically rolling her eyes. Jesse burst out laughing. Mrs Vermaak was clearly from a different generation where Englishmen were only snow white. Jesse did not have the heart to re-educate her now at this stage of her life.

Finally, her sons came home and Jesse was introduced to Jan-Hendrik and Jacobus. They were big burly men who, as a result of being in the vineyards all day long, were burnt red. Jacobus was the younger son and was a little shy but Jan-Hendrik seemed quite taken with Jesse. He offered to take Jesse around the farm. "That would be lovely but I'm afraid I'm going to have to ask you to take me back to *Sonder Moeite* instead. Josh must be worried. I didn't even let him know where I was all afternoon," she added perplexed. "Oh dear me, it's all my fault. I spoke too much all afternoon. Jan-Hendrik, please take Jesse home. We don't want trouble with the Englishman," she conceded lifting her tone deliberately. Jesse couldn't help noticing that Mrs Vermaak referred to *Sonder Moeite* as her home. She thanked Mrs Vermaak for a lovely afternoon and departed with Jan-Hendrik. Jan-Hendrik tried to be charming and made small talk with Jesse along the way. He asked her if she'd like to go with him to the last day of the festival. Jesse declined saying that she was in fact a guest of Josh Bolton. Although secretly, this was not her real reason, she actually found Jan-Hendrik a bit boorish and she preferred a more sophisticated type of man.

They arrived at *Sonder Moeite* at around six o'clock. Jesse waved goodbye to Jan-Hendrik and ran up the steps. The front door was open and as she walked in Josh came out of the living room. He was livid! "Where the hell have you been!" he boomed. "I was at Geluks Gedacht with Mrs Vermaak. I…, I'm sorry I meant to call you," she stammered. "You're sorry! You're sorry?" he asked sarcastically. "You're lying!" he accused her. "Why would I lie about where I've been," she challenged. "I went looking for you Jesse and someone told me that they saw you walk off with Phil. Didn't I tell you '*I'd see you later* '" he was shouting at her with anger and frustration. Jesse did not answer him immediately. She waited for Beth to leave the dining area where she was setting the table. "Firstly, I am not a liar," she responded emphatically, "secondly, I did not leave with Phil," she added even more calmly, "and thirdly, Mrs Vermaak invited me for tea and she wouldn't take no for an answer." "So Mrs Vermaak trapped you?" "No Josh!" she signaled impatiently, "she took me by the hand and pulled me to her car. She is a very persistent woman. She also promised that we would call you from her house but she spoke so much that we both forgot to call. And that's the truth," affirmed Jesse. "Really," Josh sneered disbelievingly. "Yes, really Joshua! I haven't seen Phil since you were so rude to him!" She caught him off-guard again when she mentioned his full name. Something inside of him seemed to soften a little. "I was very worried Jesse. Don't do that ever again," he commanded. She smiled secretly. "You were worried about me Joshua?" she asked, innocently tilting her head ever so slightly to one side. Her hair cascading forward making her seem completely irresistible.

He knew she was taunting him. Josh stepped forward and pulled her towards him. He gazed deep into her eyes and her resolve started to melt. Josh planted his lips on hers and kissed her with such intense passion and urgency that by the time he pulled away, Jesse was gasping for air. When she got her breath back, she asked, "What was that for?" "To remind you never to fool around with me again!" he replied. "I'm hungry, I haven't eaten all day. Let's eat," he instructed. She was amazed at him. "You can speak about food directly after you assault me?" "Assault you? You were asking for that!" He grabbed her arm and pulled her into the dining room. He pulled a chair out from the table and plonked her down ungracefully. "Now we must eat." The food was warm and smelt delicious and Jesse realized that she was in fact quite hungry.

Josh was relieved that she was home safe and even more glad that she had not spent the afternoon with Phil. When he came down from the auction stage and saw her empty seat a panic set into his heart but he could not let her know that he was concerned about her. He did not want her to know that he had searched all over for her at the festival. He had cross-questioned poor Phil demanding to know where Jesse was. However, the poor accused knew nothing. Josh nearly socked him. He would have made a complete fool of himself and possibly faced criminal charges had he done so. What was it about Jesse Kearns that got him so riled that he couldn't even eat all day?

Chapter Seven

It was Sunday, the last day that Jesse would be in *Robertson*. She really didn't feel like going to the festival today. Fortunately, there would be no auction so it meant that Josh also didn't have to be there early. Jesse lingered in bed, drifting in and out of sleep. Eventually she decided that it was time to get up, bath and pack. She had a long drive back to Cape Town.

By the time Jesse came downstairs it was already ten o'clock. Breakfast was served in the dining room. "Good morning Ms Kearns," greeted Beth while she poured Jesse's coffee. "Good morning Beth. Is Mr Bolton in the vineyards today?" she enquired. "No, he's still in bed. I think he's taking the day off today," she laughed. Jesse was in high spirits today. She wondered if Josh was capable of '*taking the day off*'. Jesse was midway into her breakfast when Josh came into the dining room. "Good morning, sweetheart," he greeted cheerfully, wearing a red and brown silk robe. Jesse blushed, hoping that Beth hadn't heard him call her '*Sweetheart*'. "Good morning Josh," she answered shyly. She had never seen him wearing sleepwear before and she had to admit to herself that he looked dressed for an important occasion. She scrutinized him from under her lashes and decided that it must be the way he carried himself that made him seem so dignified and important. "Would you be interested in going with me to the festival just to collect some documentation? I'm not working today." "Oh, sure I'd like that." She hesitated at first. "I hope you haven't forgotten to arrange for your driver to take me back to Cape Town," queried Jesse expectantly. "My driver won't be taking you," he pointed out. "But…"

"I'll be taking you." That whimsical smile hovered again at the corner of his mouth. "Oh." Jesse was very surprised. "Then we'd better get going," she said worriedly. "There's plenty of time," he drawled, "I'll be flying you back." Jesse was stunned. "You have an aeroplane?" "Yes, most farmers have a two-seater light aircraft. It's very convenient," he answered coolly. Jesse was gob smacked. She couldn't believe that Josh could fly an aeroplane. 'Was there anything that this man couldn't do,' she thought. He was so casual about owning an aeroplane. He spoke as if it were similar to having a bicycle parked in the garage as a trouble-free convenience. "So when do we leave then?" she asked excitedly. "Don't worry there's plenty of time. Now eat your breakfast." As usual, she obliged him – this seeming to become the nature of their relationship.

They arrived at the festival shortly after eleven o'clock. People were greeting and congratulating Josh as they walked to the offices next to the stage. "Nice work Josh!" shouted a man. Josh waved at him and smiled showing his brilliant white teeth. Jesse looked up at him wonderingly. She could see why everyone was so impressed with him. He looked like a bronze athlete. His arms tanned and sturdy; able to protect or carry any woman he desired. However, sadly, not many people saw what she had already witnessed. He could be kind yet cruel and calculating. She already regretted giving herself to him. But every time she was in his presence, she couldn't resist him. He made her feel helpless yet wanted. Was there something wrong with feeling that way? 'Of course there was,' she thought. She had interviewed many educated and established women who had given up their lives for men like Joshua Bolton. Many had lived in abusive marriages for decades shrouding their love and hurt with extreme measures of dignity. She did not want to be one of those women. She wanted a plain simple and uncomplicated life. A more predictable man would have … 'What on earth was she talking about?' she checked herself. She had merely had a brief fantasy about Josh and she was already framing the picture. 'Get a grip Jesse Kearns!' she said to herself. She knew that Joshua Bolton was not the man for her. Her grandmother would certainly not have approved. She saw how much her own father had hurt her mother. Her grandmother would certainly have wanted a more dependable and likeable man for Jesse.

Jesse dawdled outside the office while Josh signed forms and collected the necessary documentation of the previous day's auction, which he had to forward to the wine co-operative. While she waited, a number of men walking pass her tried to either make eye contact with her or hit on her. Josh came out unexpectedly while a twenty something year-old was hitting on Jesse, trying to get her telephone number. Josh took a few long strides towards the young man, his chest inflated and his clenched jaw pulsating. "Can I help you?" he thundered. The young man was certainly surprised but challenged him arrogantly. "What's it to you old boy?" Josh grabbed him by the collar, turned him around and pushed him away, saying, "Hit the road jackass!" The young man was so embarrassed that he fled. Jesse was shocked at Josh's behaviour. By now, she had turned crimson but because of her dark tan, it showed as a deep red hue. "You're okay?" he asked. Jesse nodded. Josh took her hand in his and held it tightly as they walked away. Jesse was embarrassed but felt strangely safe and protected too. Her hand was in his. She liked this feeling.

Josh opened his vehicle's door and helped Jesse in. He got in beside her and leaned over towards her, cupping her chin in his strong hand. He looked deep into Jesse's eyes and she saw that unmistakable look again. "What is it Joshua?" she asked. "Nothing!" He closed his eyes and his lips found hers once more. She tasted sweet as cherries. Jesse knew that people were watching them in the car park. But, she couldn't stop herself. Today was her last time with this oddly attractive man. And he kissed so well… Josh placed his arm around her drawing her closer into him. "I want all of you," he whispered. Oh dear… Jesse was drowning again, her resolve weakening by the second. He kissed her so tenderly and made her feel so wanted. "Do you have to go back?" he moaned. "Yes, you know I have to," she responded in between kisses. "I want you back as soon as possible, okay." Jesse drew back and shot him a surprised look. "What do you mean?" "Come back next weekend. Please..." There was an unmistakable yearning in his voice or could it have been a lonely desperation in the way he said '*Please*'?

"I have a job Josh and besides *Robertson* is quite far to have to drive to every weekend from Cape Town," she added. "I'm not asking you to come every weekend, I'm asking you to come next weekend. The festival will be over and I'll be able to devote more time to you. And besides, it won't be a three hour drive."

"What do you mean?" "Well if I fetch you with my plane it will be less than half an hour," he said coaxingly. "Really, only half an hour?" He nodded, "Maybe less. So…?"

"Alright then, I'll come back next weekend."

"Great! It's settled then. I'll fetch you at your flat with a rented car and then we'll fly back from the nearest airstrip." With those words, Josh started the vehicle and slid out of the parking lot towards *Sonder Moeite*.

This was the most exciting day of Jesse's life. She felt like a teenager again sitting next to Josh in his two-seater tomahawk aeroplane with flames painted on the sides. She had to put headphones on to drown out the noise of the engines. He flew at a very low altitude so that she could see all the towns beneath them. It was beautiful. Jesse could see people's houses and children playing in their backyards. They flew over a field with children playing football and they stopped playing in order to wave at the plane. Jesse waved back and they pointed at her and started running after the flying aeroplane. She laughed aloud, 'This is so much fun,' she thought. Josh turned and smiled at her. He looked at her lovingly. She seemed so carefree and innocent and he almost felt guilty about drawing her into his complicated life.

They were hardly up in the air when he started the gradual descent to the airstrip. Josh maneuvered the plane, landing it smoothly on the runway. Jesse was very impressed but also disappointed that the flight was over so quickly. He noticed her frame of mind instantly. "Don't worry sweetheart, I'll be flying you again on Friday. But this time I'm taking you to a different height of rapture," he added cunningly. He had a wicked look in his eyes and that unmistakable dimple gave away his impious thoughts. Josh dropped Jesse off in front of her flat. He refused to come in knowing what would happen if he did. He would undress her and ravish her all night long. The mere thought of her made him get hard.

Jesse was finally alone in her flat and everything seemed unnaturally quiet. She had become accustomed to hearing the housekeeper, Beth bustling about in the kitchen or dusting and cleaning in some room or other at *Sonder Moeite*. Now she was alone and somehow it just didn't seem right. She unpacked her bags and chose her clothes for the following day. She ran a bath for herself and climbing into the bubbles she lay there thinking about her weekend. It seemed that her tea with Mrs Vermaak happened just a short while ago. She laughed aloud when she thought of how angry Josh got when she came back from visiting Mrs Vermaak at *Geluks Gedacht*. Then there was Beth winning second place for her jam in the preserve competition, which was so affirming for her. And poor Phil, who was brushed aside like some discarded object by the rich and charming Joshua Bolton. Jesse wondered how he managed to be so likable to some yet so brusque to others. A lot had actually happened this weekend and slowly but surely, she realized that she had been drawn into Josh's world and had made friends with the people surrounding him and they in turn seemed to be quite accepting of her.

Joshua flew home back to *Robertson* with a heavy heart. He had never met a woman who intrigued him as much as Jesse Kearns. She was so petite and beautiful, yet so astonishingly unaware of these attributes. When she spoke and she tilted her head ever so slightly to the side with her long dark tendrils cascading forward in an attempt to cajole him, oh boy was he swept away. It was a constant battle for him to see her with reasonable eyes. He thought about how he had taken her just two nights ago. He had made passionate love to her and she was so accepting of him taking charge and leading the way. Her body fitted him perfectly and the very thought of her lying naked next to him amplified his breath and made him lust after her again. Sometimes she angered him, deliberately he thought. No woman had ever challenged or questioned him before. He had never tolerated that kind of thing. 'Nip it in the bud' before they came too close or got too demanding. That had always been his policy. But this time round it hadn't worked for him. She always seemed innocent or naïve and he could never figure out her motives. He thought of getting to know her better but it was too risky. He had already revealed too much of himself. He didn't really know what she was capable of as a woman or as a journalist. Only time would tell. However, being a journalist, he had to assume that a good story would give her more credibility in the news world and would encourage her to betray him in an instant in order to be the first to publish what she discovered. He couldn't risk her finding out or it might ruin him forever.

Chapter Eight

The week at the Cape Town Post was unusually hectic. There was a nationwide strike looming in the essential service sector. This meant that Jesse was diploid out of the office most of the time. She had to interview labour ministers, union officials and striking professionals such as nurses and teachers. She spent her days rushing through traffic, keeping appointments and then rushing back to the office to write her articles and forward them to the editors before the four o'clock deadlines. She was breathless and so busy that she often forgot to eat. Nevertheless, Jesse thrived on this kind of pressure. She always believed that hard work made the day go by faster and that she was making a valuable contribution to bringing up to date, groundbreaking news to the public.

Josh did not call her all week. She found this rather odd. Sometimes he gave her the impression that he was interested in her and when she expected some kind of feedback, there was just none forthcoming. He raised her expectations and then just left her hanging. Jesse didn't want to call Josh. She didn't want to appear desperate for his company but she kept checking her mobile phone for new messages. He really was a dark horse. By late Thursday afternoon, Jesse was so tired that she hoped Friday would come sooner. She was actually looking forward to the weekend in quiet *Robertson*.

Finally, it was Friday and Jesse worked in her lunch hour in order to leave a little earlier. She cleared her desk and checked with Mitch if he wanted her to complete any last minute work. "Are you still here?" Mitch asked. "You've worked very hard this week Jesse, you deserve this break. And if that Bolton guy tries anything weird with you, let me know. I'll fly up there in my plane and fix him personally," he mocked. Mitch's appreciation of her confirmed that she wouldn't want to work for anyone else. "Well if that's all, then I guess I'm out of here," she responded wearily.

Just twenty minutes later Jesse was in her flat packing her bag for the weekend. She was not even sure what time Josh would be here. He still had not called. She washed her face and refreshed her makeup. Just then, the buzzer rang. She picked up the intercom phone and saw him standing there in his denims and T-shirt. Her heart flipped. Jesse buzzed Josh in. She opened her front door just as he reached it. He leaned against the doorframe, the light from outside illuminating his imposing frame. He stood there taking all of her in admiringly. "Hello," she greeted, shyly aware of him. He smiled and said, "If you're ready, let's go." She felt slighted. No hug, no kiss, no 'I'm glad to see you.' But she held her head high and pretended to be just as casual and nonchalant as she walked out the door.

Josh packed Jesse's bags into the rental car and opened the passenger door for her. He sped away rather fast and Jesse stole a glance at him. Damn, he was a fine looking man, she thought to herself. "Are we late?" asked Jesse looking at the speedometer. "No my love, but the quicker we get there the more time I have to spend with you. It seemed like it was going to be a wonderful weekend. Josh was in a good mood. They arrived at the two-seater aircraft in record time. Josh's tomahawk aeroplane stood waiting on the deserted runway. Jesse could feel the excitement welling up inside of her. She loved flying with Josh. He seemed so utterly in control of the aeroplane and of her destiny. She secretly wished he could fly her to some forbidden destination.

Josh flew at a slightly higher altitude this time because she could not make out people or buildings as clearly as she could the last time. The coastline also seemed to stretch on forever. Suddenly she realized that they should have been flying inland because Robertson was quite far from the coastline. "Why are we not flying inland?"

"Don't worry," he said with a whimsical smile at the corner of his mouth. Jesse wondered what Josh was up to this time. Soon enough they began their descent. As soon as they touched the ground, Josh taxied the aeroplane down the runway. Jesse looked out of the window and saw a '*Welcome to Plettenberg Bay*' sign on the airport building. "Joshua!" she exclaimed excitedly. Plettenberg Bay was known to be the playground of the rich and famous. Every time Jesse called him with his full name, something inside of him somersaulted. He looked at her with such admiration. Josh slowly brought the aeroplane to a standstill and turned to Jesse cupping her face in his large hands. Whenever he looked into her almond smoky eyes, he felt as if he could drown in them. She was truly beautiful. She astounded him. He leaned over and pulled her nearer as gently as ever and he kissed her tenderly. Jesse responded without thinking. His mouth was warm and inviting and she could do nothing but accept the invitation. He kissed her lips and the line of her neck passionately and then he worked his magic on her earlobes nibbling and kissing them. "I've missed you so much, Jesse Kearns," he crooned breathlessly. The Josh Bolton who drew her was back. "This was the longest week of my life," he continued. "You missed me but you didn't even call", responded Jesse hurt. "If I had called you it would have intensified the longing. I would have been forced to come to Cape Town and make a nuisance of myself."

"You could never be a nuisance, Josh," she protested emphatically. He kissed her again and then forced himself to get out.

"Come, let's begin the weekend," he said opening the aircraft door. Josh jumped out, walked around the plane and opened the passenger door for Jesse. He didn't bother to put the stepladder out for her. Instead, he held out his arms and she jumped into his hold squealing with delight. He held her close and said. "Jesse Kearns, I intend to give you the best weekend of your life." "You wicked, wicked man!" she laughed. He held her hand as though he'd never let go of her.

They walked towards the airport building and Jesse saw a black limousine standing on the runway. "Someone famous or important must be coming," said Jesse pointing to the Limousine. "Yes, someone very important," agreed Josh walking towards the Limousine. The chauffer was already standing outside holding the back passenger door open. Jesse was stunned. She turned to Josh but before she could say anything, he smiled and said, "Ladies first." Jesse climbed into the beautiful leather interior. There was a bottle of chilled sparkling fruit juice, a bouquet of roses and a romantic love ballad playing in the background. Josh got in beside her and the Limousine cruised away silently with the two lovebirds. "Oh, Joshua! Is this all for me?" "You deserve more my love. I've been a jerk but I intend to make it up to you." Jesse tilted her head ever so slightly allowing her hair to cascade forward, "You mean, you'll be my slave this weekend?" she questioned wickedly. He laughed. "Your wish is my command."

This was wild. Nobody had ever done anything this nice for her in the past. Joshua Bolton rose a couple of notches in her book. If he treated her, this well, then he definitely qualified. This was going to be a fantastic weekend. Jesse snuggled closer to him on the large leather seat of the Limousine and Josh put his arm around her pulling her closer to him. She didn't want to ask where they were going, too afraid that the spell would be broken and she'd wake up finding herself sitting in a pumpkin.

The limousine whisked them away to the famous Plettenberg Beach Hotel. She could see it perched in the distance, seeming to be stranded in the middle of the sea. The sea kept making a half hearted attempt to swallow it up. It was a splendid building. The limousine stopped at the entrance of the hotel and a bellman stood ready to open their door. Josh got out first and held his hand out for Jesse. He nodded to the bellman and they walked into the hotel. "Do you mind waiting in the living room while I check in," he asked. Jesse sat in the most luxurious autumn coloured chair. There were many wealthy looking people dripping in diamonds who seemed to be going about their daily business of relaxing and enjoying life without a care in the world. She wondered how meaningful one's existence could be, being on a constant holiday. Soon Josh came towards her followed by a bellhopper who had their luggage on a trolley. They stood in a lift going up to the third floor. The lift was more luxurious than her entire flat in Cape Town. It had carpeted walls, fibre optic lights, and the most beautiful baroque music coming from somewhere. As they stepped out, Josh opened an apartment door and she stepped into a wonderland. There was a four-poster bed at one end of the room with a living room leading off it. The balcony doors were open. Hanging on the doorframe were white organza curtains blowing lazily in the sea breeze. Her feet sank nearly ankle deep in carpet as she stepped into the room. There was a welcome bowl of fruit, chocolates and champagne, flower petals scattered on the bed and vases filled with all kinds of beautiful blooms. Jesse didn't even know the names of the blossoms. The air was heavy with their aromatic scent. All she could say was, "Oh my word! I'm in heaven!" Josh smiled and mused, "I hope this is up to standard, Ms Kearns." "Well, they could have put more flowers and perhaps my own personal maid would have given my stamp of approval," she complained disapprovingly, shaking her head. She laughed aloud when she saw the look on Josh's face. "Joshua, it is more than I ever dreamed of. Thank you so much." He smiled and pulled her close to him. Jesse knew how to make him feel wanted and appreciated. "There is one thing though," he added. "What is it Josh?" "We have adjoining rooms, in case you wanted your privacy." "Oh! Well, I'll just have to come and creep into your room at the dead of night when nobody is looking," she wheedled him cunningly. "I won't tell, if you don't tell," he teased. It was settled then; they were both going to have a marvelous time. "I'll give you time to unpack and I'll meet you down stairs for dinner in an hour," he said leaving the room. Jesse looked around her and smiled. Why was Josh being so thoughtful? He seemed more than nice to her. What might she do or say to turn him into an unforgivable monster again? She felt almost afraid that she would do something unintentional and break the spell.

Well as Josh had gone out of his way to make this a special weekend for her, the least she could do was spruce herself up a little to suit the occasion. Jesse unpacked a long blue dress that she had only worn once and placed it on the bed. She had a quick shower and moisturized her soft tan skin. She slipped the dress on and the diamantes on the dress seemed to tumble down her bosom and come to a halt at her navel. This evening she decided to wear her hair up. She pinned her locks into a French knot with fine tendrils cascading around her face framing her beautiful features. She lined her eyes with a black kohl pencil and put just a dash of mauve lipstick on. Pressing her lips together, she was grateful for the fact that her features were accentuated with just the tiniest bit of make up. Jesse perfumed herself at strategic points and eyed herself appreciatively in the long mirror. Finally, she slipped on a pair of delicate silver sandals and picked up her purse. She was ready for Joshua Bolton.

Jesse stepped out of the lift and entered the lobby that ran directly into the sunken dining area. She stood for a second at the top step to appraise the view and then gently lowered her leg to the next step. A room full of eyes lowered to her leg, which peeped out of the long slit in her dress. The maître d' led her to where Josh was seated. Heads turned as she passed and some people stopped talking to their companions in mid sentence, their eyes following her. Josh could not help noticing all the attention she drew. He stood up as she came towards him, took her hand and lifted it to his lips. "Jesse Kearns, you are truly a welcome sight. I feel like the luckiest man alive," he whispered proudly. Jesse smiled charmingly and slid into her seat opposite him. Josh felt so fortunate to be the one seated opposite her.

A waiter served wine and sparkling fruit juice. The two made light conversation by the glow of the candlelight until the food came. Then Jesse enquired, "Josh, do I look okay?" "Well in Cornwall we would have said, 'Jesse Kearns, you look darn smashing! Why?" "I've noticed people looking at me all evening."

"I think it's because they can't believe that someone so beautiful would mind being seated next to someone so ugly," he laughed. "There can be some improvement, but you're not so bad," she teased. He looked at her, holding his chest in mock hurt. Josh studied her silently, taking in her silky soft brown skin. He noticed how her bosom heaved quietly with each heartbeat and when she turned to look at him unexpectedly, he conveniently dropped his napkin and had to retrieve it. As he bent down to pick it up, and saw her long toned leg peeping out of the slit in the blue dress, Josh was lost. He wondered where Jesse had been all his life. She looked so calm and relaxed and he really wanted this weekend to be special for her.

"So what was your week like?" he enquired caringly. "Well, you've heard about the strike in the services sector – Mitch had me out in the field interviewing strikers, union members and government officials." "It must have been quite hectic?" "Yes, I was running between interviews and the office to get my deadlines out on time. I actually forgot to eat sometimes, can you believe that?" she said surprised at herself. "Well, you'll just have to make up for lost food now," he returned, just as the waiter wheeled the dessert cart in. Her favourite part of the meal had arrived - dessert. The melted cream and chocolate was like heaven. Jesse's tongue feasted on the sensual flavours exploding on her palate. She listened attentively to Josh between mouthfuls as he spoke about the new cabernet he was producing. He was so good looking. She contemplated what was hiding behind those hazel eyes. That troubled look had disappeared but she wondered what it was that brought it on.

The dinner band started playing and Jesse was suddenly distracted. Josh noticed her turning to look at the band and took it as a cue. He got up and offered her his hand. "Would you dance with me, please?" Everything seemed to melt away. Jesse smiled and inwardly she was glowing. She loved to dance; after all she was from Cape Town. Josh twirled her onto the dance floor and held her like a professional. He took her straight into a waltz and was pleasantly surprised that she danced so well. Jesse positioned herself perfectly into his body. The music took her away to a distant land. By now, people in the dining area had turned their seats to watch the two and when the music gently faded away and the dance ended, people clapped for them. Josh was not at all perturbed although Jesse's cheeks turned a flaming red. He was in his element as he had promised to make this weekend perfect for her. The beat of the music picked up to an Argentinean tango. Josh whisked Jesse across the floor stopping intermittently to shake his head. It was beautiful to watch. After the dance, he thanked her and walked her back to her seat. Jesse was glowing. She drank to quench her thirst as the other patrons took to the floor for a slow foxtrot. "I didn't know you danced so well?" she teased, her tendrils casting a shadow over her mocking smile. "Oh! The lady thinks I dance well. In that case let me take you for the dance of love." He later lured her into the dance of love – the rumba. When they entered the dance floor, the people made way for them. The enchanted crowd surrounded the two lovebirds. It was an extremely intense dance. Josh showed his passion for her quite publicly. His eyes smoldered when he gazed at her, burning through her soul. He wanted her and she made it obvious by the movements of her body that she was not easy. Towards the end, he worked his magic like a prince trying to win his princess. The dance ended with Josh's lips just millimeters away from Jesse's. The two of them locked in a wanton embrace oblivious of the clapping crowd. It was a magical night!

They entered their room exhausted but elated. "Joshua, I had a fantastic time! Thank you, I'll always remember tonight." "Don't thank me yet. The night is still young my love. Just remember there's more where that came from," he added laughingly. Joshua's mobile phone rang and he excused himself and went into his adjoining room without closing the door. Jesse heard him talking business on the phone and he sounded quite agitated. She prepared herself for an invigorating shower while Joshua seemed to be trying to work something out over the phone. She thought about the wonderful evening as she lathered herself with lavender scented soap. Jesse came out of the bathroom with a towel draped around her and still Josh was on the phone. She heard his raised voice and she wondered what the problem was. After she had dressed into her negligee, she got into bed and put the television on.

Soon Josh came out of the adjoining room. He seemed quite perturbed. "Sorry, I was on the phone so long." "Is everything alright?" she asked concerned. "No, one of the wine vats is leaking and I tried to get a welder to fix it before the problem gets out of control. The only problem is that it is the cabernet wine I've been working on for so long." Jesse could see that he was worried. "Joshua, if you need to go back to the farm then its okay, I understand." He bent over close to her on the bed, cupped her face in his strong hands and gazed deep into her eyes. "Jesse, I'm sorry that this had to happen but we are going to enjoy ourselves. There's always next year for another superb wine. Right now you are more important to me." This Englishman had completely won Jesse's heart. He had put her right at the top of his agenda. No one had ever made her feel so special. But she didn't want him to be with her while having a worry in the back of his mind. "Joshua, perhaps you could fly back home early tomorrow morning and then sort out the problem and then maybe you could be back by lunch time." He considered her suggestion briefly. "Are you sure you're okay with that?"

"Absolutely, just make sure you come back." "Nothing will keep me from you, Jesse Kearns. I'll arrange for you to be pampered tomorrow morning in the hotel's plush spa, while I'm away. That will keep you busy and prevent you from missing me too much," he added jokingly. Jesse shrieked with delight. It was settled then. Josh called reception and made a booking for Jesse at the hotel spa.

It had been a long day but it was some time before Josh came to bed and Jesse was already sound asleep. He curled up beside her and wrapped her in his arms. Both of them were exhausted and soon all that came from their lips was their steady peaceful breathing.

When Jesse awoke, Josh had already gone. He left a note at her bedside. She picked it up and read... *'You look beautiful when you sleep. Enjoy breakfast and the pampering. Will see you at lunch. Love Josh.* The words *'love Josh'* were written in a long bold drawled handwriting. Jesse picked up the hotel phone and called for room service. While she waited, she read the note over and over again. What did *'love Josh'* mean? Was he saying that he loved her or was he merely passing on his best wishes to her. With Joshua Bolton, one never really knew where one stood. In any event, the note was the only piece of evidence she had to prove that this dark Englishman existed. Jesse tucked the note into her purse.

Breakfast was scrumptious and soon after, Jesse made her way down to the hotel spa to spend a morning of luxury. The spa was plush. There were thick expensive towels on the massage tables and the dimly lit room was scented with aromatherapy oils and candles. A masseuse pampered Jesse from head to toe. She relished in the body scrub and the massage. The pampering ended with her toes where her feet were massaged, then pedicured. At first, Jesse refused the French nails. Instead, a nail technician painted them a deep golden brown to match her skin. Jesse was in another world entirely. After the pampering, she felt like a brand new person. She left the spa reluctantly and went to sit at the pool sipping a fruit cocktail. This was really a good life and she felt truly blessed to have been given such an opportunity. Now to complete it, Joshua needed to come back.

Soon he appeared, just as though she had telepathically summoned him to her side. Jesse smiled when she felt his presence. He kissed her long and tenderly on the lips. "I've been gone too long my love." "But I'm glad you're back Josh," she added perkily. "Did you manage to sort out the problem?" "Yes, Jaco has everything under control now and the welder has welded the two leaks. It seems that the consignment of wine was saved," he added relieved. "I've also instructed them not to phone me again. That includes Jaco and Beth." Jesse was glad that he had gone to the farm. At least she had all of him back and not half of him with her and the other half, worrying about the problems on the farm. "You know Josh, I'm so glad you have an aeroplane." "Why?" he enquired curiously. "Well now I can send you to Paris to buy me a bottle of perfume," she laughed teasingly. "Bring it on Jackie 'O', Aristotle is at your service." That's what she loved so much about Joshua. He knew exactly what she was talking about. They were completely in sync with each other.

Josh stood up and pulled Jesse to her feet. He looked at her and Jesse knew what his intentions were. He kissed her passionately, searching her mouth. "I want you Jesse Kearns" "Joshua, there are people around," she was embarrassed. He didn't bother to respond but scooped her up in his arms and carried her into the hotel. In the lift, he became frantic, kissing her and caressing her soft perky breasts. Upon entering their hotel room, he flung the door open with her in his arms and kicked it closed with his foot. Josh gracefully lowered Jesse on the bed and then himself on top of her and made passionate love to her. "Oh Joshua!" Jesse kept calling his name. He responded to the longing in her and filled her with a joy she had only

71

experienced once before with him at *Sonder Moeite*. When he had finished satisfying her, Josh rolled over to look at her. She looked like a bronzed goddess waiting to devour him. Josh loved it when Jesse initiated the lovemaking. She wasn't shy and gave him just as much pleasure as he had given her. After a while, they turned round, clasped each other and fell soundly asleep.

The weekend in Plettenberg bay was marvelous. When Josh and Jesse were not in their hotel they were either soaking up the gorgeous sun or swimming at the beach or taking long strolls hand in hand on the warm soft sea sand. It was so interesting for Jesse to get to know Josh outside of the farming community. He was different. Not only was he handsome and charming but kind and considerate as well. He in turn found her to be intelligent and deep. She was knowledgeable about most of the topics he introduced. Most of the women from his past were superficial and only after his money and a good time. He had found his equal in Jesse.

However, all good things had to end and soon it was time to fly back to *Sonder Moeite*. Their bags were packed and Josh lifted Jesse into his two-seater tomahawk aeroplane. He started the engine and cruised swiftly down the runway urging the aeroplane to lift its nose and fly off into the deep blue sky. Jesse turned to look behind her and all she could see was the hotel abandoned in the middle of the ocean.

Chapter Nine

The sun was setting as Josh taxied the aircraft into the barn, which doubled as the aeroplane hanger. He loaded their luggage into his 4x4 vehicle and drove back to *Sonder Moeite,* which was a short distance away. The house seemed unusually quiet as he put the luggage in the hallway. "Beth!" he called. "It seems we have the house to ourselves," he turned to Jesse with a wicked glint in his eyes and that unmistakable dimple taunting her. "Mr Bolton…Sir," stammered Beth coming nervously out of an adjoining room. "Beth, what is it?" She looked pale and worried. "Beth are you alright?" asked Jesse concerned. "Oh she's alright!" mocked a high-pitched voice coming down the stairs. Josh's whole body stiffened. Jesse looked at him confused. His worst nightmare had come true. The woman standing on the bottom stairs was tall and slender. She had on an elegantly tailored grey suit. She had large emerald green eyes and thick-cropped black hair, cut expertly into the nape of her long elegant neck. Her red lips were thin and tensed as she smiled mockingly with a raised eyebrow at Josh. "Josh darling, tell her who I am." Josh's jaw was twitching uncontrollably and his anger was visibly rising. "What the hell are you doing here, Ava?" he stormed towards her. For a split-second, Ava looked frightened and took a step back up. Josh's mind was racing. Everything was going so well with him and Jesse and he didn't want to lose her. Not now…

"Joshua, what is going on? Who is this woman?" implored Jesse. "You must be the new woman in Josh's life," butted in Ava. For the second time in his life, Joshua Bolton was cornered. He had to come clean at the risk of losing Jesse, something he was trying to avoid from the start. He turned to face Jesse. "Please try to understand that I never meant to hurt you." "Joshua, what are you saying?" Jesse felt the ground shake underneath her. Somehow, she felt that she was standing on a precipice with a monster behind her. If she jumped she was doomed, if she stayed to face the monster she was doomed too.

73

"Who is this woman?" she repeated. "Ava is my wife…" "What!" Jesse turned her face away from him as if his words had slapped her. Time seemed to stand still. The atmosphere turned cold. A knife could cut the tension in the air. "It's not what you think, Jesse." "This is your wife… what am I supposed to think?" she choked on her words. She turned and ran blindly out of the house into the twilight evening. "No, Jesse wait, please!" Josh called after her. All she kept hearing was Ava's shrill mocking laughter behind her. She just kept running. She ran and ran down the Jacaranda tree lined driveway. The evening was already cold but she couldn't feel anything. Her legs felt like heavy stumps. By now, she had reached the main road. Suddenly she stumbled and fell. She tried to get up but her legs wouldn't move so she just lay there in the long damp grass on the side of the road. After a long while, she remembered her mobile phone was in her pocket. She took it out and decided to call someone to come and fetch her. Then, she realized that she was far away from home, from Cape Town. Who could she call to come and fetch her? Jesse's mind was racing; she started to feel cold and was suddenly afraid. Just then, she remembered Mrs Vermaak and dialed her number. Jesse was hysterical on the phone and couldn't exactly describe what had happened to her.

It wasn't long before she saw the headlights of Jan-Hendrik's vehicle and she knew she would be safe. Jan-Hendrik helped her into the front seat. "Are you alright, Jesse?" he asked in his mother's concerned Afrikaans accent. She nodded, unable to say more. As soon as they got to *Geluks Gedacht*, Jan-Hendrik helped her into the house. Mrs Vermaak was already waiting with a steaming cup of tea. "My goodness child, are you alright?" she fussed. "Jan-Hendrik, please leave us!" she ordered. He obeyed his mother without saying a word. Mrs Vermaak took a knitted shawl and draped it over Jesse's shivering shoulders and poured her a hot cup of tea. "Here, my dear, this will make you feel better," she said handing Jesse the steaming cup of tea. She waited patiently for Jesse to calm down. As the colour started returning to Jesse's face, she asked gently, "What happened child?" "Joshua Bolton's wife is here," she uttered calmly. The words sounded strange to her and she didn't recognize her own voice. She repeated herself. "Joshua Bolton has a wife," as if saying it again would convince her. Mrs Vermaak's jaw had dropped. Just then, the telephone rang and Mrs Vermaak answered it in her typical high-pitched falsetto voice. "*Geluks Gedacht,* good evening..." "Mrs Vermaak, Josh Bolton here. Have you seen Jesse Kearns?" "Jesse is here but I warn you, Englishman, I have ordered my staff to shoot any trespassers on *Geluks Gedacht*!" she blurted out slamming the phone down. She turned to Jesse, "he knows you are here but don't worry, Jan-Hendrik will shoot him if he comes onto my property," she stated emphatically.

Mrs Vermaak could see that not only was Jesse heartbroken but also in shock. She spoke very kindly to her and explained to Jesse about the perils of love. "Sometimes, when we are in love Jesse, there is no logic or reason or even time. The heart wants what the heart wants," said Mrs Vermaak comfortingly. She looked wistfully ahead as if she was remembering someone from her own past. Later when Jesse was calmer, she took her upstairs into one of her guest rooms. It was a beautiful room with lots of lace, beads and trimmings. It looked like the décor style out of a 1920's or 1930's movie. She tucked Jesse into bed and handed her a tot of brandy in warm milk saying, "drink up child, this is an old Cape Dutch remedy for the nerves. It will help you to sleep."

Jesse woke up at around eight o'clock the next morning to find a warm cup of coffee at her bedside. She was slightly confused when she saw her surroundings. She sat up in bed wondering where she was and then swung her legs off the bed and when her feet touched the floor, it all came flooding back to her. In the corner of the room, she saw the luggage that she had packed in Plettenberg Bay. Jesse later found out that Jan-Hendrik had gone to collect it early in the morning at *Sonder Moeite.* Jesse got up, stepped into a warm shower, and just allowed the beads of water to caress her tan supple body. Water cascaded down her bosom where Josh's lips had been just the day before. She tried to think clearly but could not. Last night's events came crashing into her mind, replaying themselves repeatedly in her head. 'How on earth could Josh still be married?' He had seemed so honest. He was in love with her, she was so sure. Perhaps he was the kind of man who could love two women at once. It didn't make sense to her. Perhaps the signs were there but she was too distracted to notice. Then suddenly, Jesse remembered that strange troubled look Josh used to get sometimes. It must have been guilt, which the poor bastard was trying to conceal. She should stop analyzing her situation and come up with a plan.

Later Jesse came downstairs to find Mrs Vermaak reading the newspaper at the dining room table. She looked up when Jesse entered. "Sleep well, child?" she asked concerned. "Yes. Thank you for your kindness and hospitality, Mrs Vermaak. I really didn't mean to intrude but I didn't know who else to call." "Don't worry Jesse; I'm glad it was me you could call on."

"I've decided to head back to Cape Town today. Would Jan-Hendrik be able to take me to the bus terminus please?" she asked. "Jan-Hendrik has already left for Swellendam to make a wine delivery and he will be back quite late. I wonder…" she thought. "Let's ask Phil McKinley." Before Jesse could answer, Mrs Vermaak was already on the phone to Phil. Jesse could hear her issuing instructions to poor Phil. She came back smiling. "It's settled. Phil will take you back at eleven o'clock." The smug look on her face told Jesse that nobody was willing or able to refuse Mrs Vermaak. "Come have some breakfast, it's a long drive back," she instructed.

Phil arrived promptly. Mrs Vermaak looked up approvingly when she heard the doorbell chime. "He's on time!..." That was all she said. Phil packed Jesse's luggage into his car. Mrs Vermaak came out with Jesse and turned to her saying, "Jesse, sometimes it is a good thing to have loved and lost than never to have loved at all. These are memories you will always have and sometimes with love comes regret but your heart will mend, my child."

"Thank you Mrs Vermaak, I will always remember you."

"Don't just remember me child, please come and visit sometimes."
"I will, I will," she called out as the car drove down the lane leaving a trail of dust and dried leaves behind.

Phil was aware that something had happened to Jesse but he didn't have the heart to ask. He tried making small talk but Jesse was far away. Eventually he stopped talking and played some light classical music, which lulled Jesse to sleep. By the time Jesse awoke, they were entering the Huguenot Toll Tunnel. The tunnel always held an aura of mystery for Jesse. It was dark yet light. It was scary yet safe. But most of all it was long yet short. Somehow, it represented her life experiences. She was strangely relieved when they exited the tunnel on the other side.

Phil dropped Jesse in front of her block of flats. He declined to come in saying, "Perhaps another time, I still have some business to take care of."

"Okay. Phil thanks very much I really appreciate it." He looked pensively at Jesse and said, "Please, look after yourself." "I will Phil, thanks. Drive safely."

Jesse unpacked her bags and made herself a hot cup of tea. She could not believe that her life had taken such an ugly turn. Josh had hid things from her from the start. It all made sense now. That was why he was so rude to her on their first meeting. He thought that she was a gossip columnist and would uncover the sordid truth about his double life. Jesse felt terribly guilty. To think that she had slept with another woman's husband. Her Grandmother would have turned in her grave had she witnessed this. She had raised Jesse to be a respectable young woman and to think that Jesse had now caused another woman so much pain. How was she going to forgive herself?

That night she slept very restlessly. Jesse tossed and turned and she dreamed that she was standing at a bonfire and a tall man with horns in his head was standing opposite her. He was dancing around the fire and every few moments he would stop, point his long bony finger at her and laugh. His long writhing body danced frenziedly around the fire and shrill laughter came from his white lips. "Ha! Ha! He! He! Haaa! Heee! Hiiii!" "No! No! Please stop!" screamed Jesse. She woke up in a pool of sweat, frightened and alone.

Chapter 10

The days were long and painful. The minutes ticked by unchallenged and whenever Jesse looked at the clock the time was still within the same hour. There was nothing for her to do but to forget Joshua Bolton and simply bury herself in her work. She worked around the clock, chasing after news making stories. Sometimes she worked hard but yielded very few results. However, most of the times she would find something very interesting to write about then had to dash back to the office to meet her deadline. Jesse was so busy that she often forgot to eat and then when she got back to her flat in the evening she was too tired to cook. Most evenings she would eat a fruit salad and yogurt or bread and tea. Her colleagues at work began to notice that she was losing weight.

Jesse did not hear from Josh again. In a way, she was very sad that he never bothered to contact her but sometimes she was grateful that he did not face her. She had no idea what she would do if he called or came to see her. Her mind was racing constantly but her heart was shattered into tiny fragments. Picking up the pieces seemed like an impossibility. Jesse tried hard not to think of Josh. It was difficult, but focusing on her work kept her thoughts occupied.

Mitch could see that Jesse was struggling and he felt so sorry for her. Mitch really adored her as if she were his own daughter and wanted her to be happy. He knew he had to broach the subject gently. "Jesse you've been working too hard, don't you think you need a break?"

"I'm fine Mitch, really," she confirmed defensively. "Well, in that case I have another assignment for you." "Really, what is it?" her face lit up. "There's an entourage of businessmen, six I think, from the Middle East coming into town. They're interested in buying some exclusive property on the Waterfront. I need you to take them around for three days."

"Three whole days?" whined Jesse. "Yes, three whole days. All you need to do is attend one or two of their meetings and then wine and dine them. Take them to lunch - show them the city. You won't be required to come into the office at all. I'll leave your portfolio as well as rental car and Diners card information, at reception." Before Jesse could respond, Mitch turned and walked out of the office. She looked at his back and whispered softly to herself, 'Thanks Mitch.'

Jesse drove the band of foreigners from the airport in a rented minibus. She couldn't make out what they were saying but there was much excitement coming from the back of the vehicle. They were pointing at Table Mountain. "Yes, Table Mountain!" shouted Jesse. "It's one of the New7Wonders of Nature". "You take us up there!" instructed a man dressed like an Arab. "Yes, but first we book into your hotel and deposit your luggage. "NO! We go now!" shouted the man waving a handful of cash at Jesse. Jesse politely and slowly drove the vehicle onto the side of the road, switched off the engine and turned around facing the foreign men. "Gentlemen, if you value your lives please put your money away and do not carry such a lot of cash on you. In this country, you could be killed for 50 cents. We will go to the hotel first, then we have lunch and lastly we go up Table Mountain in the cable car. Understood?" she declared firmly. There was silence from the back and she started up the vehicle again and headed toward the hotel.

Jesse made sure that they were all booked into a hotel on the Waterfront so that they didn't have to travel to their meetings. After a scrumptious lunch, they proceeded up Table Mountain in the cable car. There was much excitement and the Arabs flashed lots of expensive camera equipment around. Then Jesse had to get the group back to the hotel for their first meeting with a South African property investment company. She sat through the entire meeting, but was not allowed to ask questions nor take notes. Jesse found it interesting and thought that it would have been helpful to have known this information when she was writing her article on land redistribution. Suddenly she remembered Josh and realized that she hadn't thought of him all day. She smiled to herself and thought that this must be a good sign. After a delightful dinner at an exclusive hotel on the waterfront, Jesse bade her guests' goodnight and returned to her flat. For the first time in weeks, she felt that she was coping. She ran herself a full bath and soaked away for almost an hour. It was a good day; she had pleasant thoughts, two full meals and some time to process the day's events. She wondered why the Cape Town Post was picking up the tab for the meals, yet she wasn't allowed to ask questions or take notes in the meetings. She'd have to ask Mitch about that. Jesse went to bed earlier than usual and had a peaceful sleep.

On the following day, Jesse woke up early and decided to have breakfast at the hotel. Her guests were already seated when she arrived. "What we are doing today?" enquired the Turkish gentleman, accentuating his r's in broken English. "Today, I'll take you for a drive around the Peninsula so you can see all the available properties along the coastline," affirmed Jesse. "Good, good!" they all shouted in unison. That day Jesse drove her guests all around the Peninsula, stopping intermittently so that they could take in the view and take some photographs. They stopped for a traditional Fish and Calamari lunch and the men seemed thoroughly at home eating with their fingers.

On the third day, Jesse attended the obligatory meeting and met with the Turkish ambassador to South Africa. There were a lot of rituals and ceremonial customs, which amused Jesse all morning. She kept wondering how people were continually able to put up with these façades. Nonetheless, the day ended smoothly with Jesse transporting all the visitors back to the airport in time for their flights home. She popped into the office on her way from the airport to hand back the

Diners card and the receipts. "So, did you have a good time?" enquired Mitch. "Yes, it was a nice break away from the office," Jesse assured him. "And not one of the Turks wanted to take you home as a second or third wife?" asked Mitch feigning disappointment. "No Mitch, I didn't give them a chance. I laid down the law on the first day," she laughed. "Mitch, why was I given this assignment when I wasn't allowed to report on it?"

"This was a personal favour to the ambassador, a friend of mine."

"The Turkish ambassador is your friend?" questioned Jesse. "Yes, but without me he is nothing," retorted Mitch with a mock Turkish accent. "Well, I'm off. See you tomorrow," bowed Jesse with imaginary pomp and ceremony. Mitch just shook his head fondly at her.

Once she got home, Jesse realized that she hadn't brooded over Josh for three days. This was a good sign. It meant that she could now move on with her life. She was going out tonight with some girlfriends and they had planned to go dancing at some of the popular nightclubs in town. Jesse got dressed in a short black dress with spaghetti straps with her favourite black and silver dancing shoes as she grabbed her clutch bag and stuffed some money into it, her eye caught sight of a piece of paper. She unfolded it and there in bold sprawled handwriting were the words *'You look beautiful when you sleep. Enjoy breakfast and the pampering. Will see you at lunch. Love Josh.'* Jesse caught her breath. She couldn't even remember having put the note in her clutch bag. She threw it down on the bed and walked out. Josh was not going to ruin her evening. When she got downstairs, the girls were already waiting in their car. There was a lot of hooting, shrieking and laughter. "You girls are crazy! One would swear you were only freed from jail this morning," teased Jesse. "Yes we have been," shouted Amanda, "and the men better watch out tonight!" Amanda was a redhead high school friend of

Jesse's. Jesse couldn't ever recall Amanda being in a foul mood, she was an unfailing optimist ready to tackle any problem thrown at her.

The club was crowded as usual and all Jesse could think of was dancing the night away. The barman sent over a round of free drinks for the 'ladies, compliments of a certain patron' just as they seated themselves. There was one non-alcoholic sparkling fruit juice on the tray with the other alcoholic beverages. Jesse sipped it tentatively and looked around her not knowing who or what she was looking for. Something felt a bit odd to her but she couldn't place it and immediately dismissed the thought. Eventually they were all on the dance floor rocking and jiving to the pulsating music. All her woes forgotten – Jesse was really enjoying herself. One by one, a gentleman would walk up and ask her or one of her girlfriends to dance. This went on for most of the evening until Amanda came back with a guy's phone number – she was shrieking with excitement. A salsa song started playing and a good looking guy came up to Jesse to ask her for a dance. She didn't hesitate because she loved Latin music. They danced rhythmically to the music, her heart throbbing as her partner spun her around so hard and fast into another man's arms. Her head was spinning as she looked straight into Josh Bolton's glittering eyes. "What the devil…?" "Just dance, we'll talk later," he commanded. Jesse was overwhelmed with a feeling of safety, of familiarity. Was this a dream? Had her dream come true? It couldn't be a dream because she could feel his hard lean body pressing into her as he guided her expertly across the floor. He lifted her off the floor only to have her land softly next to him. Josh looked at Jesse with the longing he had looked at her with in Plettenberg Bay. She looked up at him and somehow he looked slightly older and a little tired. She could not detect that strange look he sometimes used to get.

Josh led her to her friends after the dance and announced that Jesse would be leaving with him. Amanda stood up to challenge Josh but

Jesse diffused the situation by confirming that she was okay and that she had to settle a matter that concerned them. They walked out of the nightclub into the cool evening with Jesse's ears still ringing from the loud music. Josh had parked his signature German car on the opposite side of the road. He opened the front passenger door for her and she slipped into the familiar surroundings and drove back to Jesse's flat in silence. As soon as they arrived at her flat, Jesse put the kettle on for coffee and kicked off her heels. She was all ears waiting for an explanation of what had happened that night at *Sonder Moeite*. Josh eyed her attentively looking for any sign of something but Jesse wasn't going to allow him to get into her head or her heart. This time around, she promised herself, things were going to be done properly. She definitely wasn't going to repeat her own mother's mistakes.

Chapter 11

There was a long silence while they waited for the kettle to boil. Then Jesse took two mugs off a shelf and poured the coffee. She remembered that Josh took two sugars but she stopped herself and instead took out the sugar bowl placing it on a tray. She was not going to be familiar with him. She was going to be cordial. Yes, she was going to be cordial. It was her best option. He would think that she had moved on, perhaps even met someone else and fallen in love again. Well, let's not push it she thought.

Jesse placed the coffee in front of Josh and waited for him to make the first move. "Thanks, this is just what I need," he uttered relieved. 'What you need is a hard slap,' she thought, reserving her attempts at punishment to herself. Josh set his mug down on the table and leaned forward. "Jesse, how have you been?" he asked concerned. "Joshua, please, you didn't come all the way to Cape Town to ask me how I have been," she uttered contemptuously. "No, you are right. I came here to explain to you what had happened." "What is there to explain Joshua? You are a married man who was fooling around with a single woman. It's that simple."

"Well, you're wrong Jesse. Things are not always what they seem."

"Really, well perhaps I need my head read then," she answered sarcastically. "Jesse, I entered an arranged marriage with Ava. My family was in financial trouble. My father had mismanaged the family funds and the management of the estate. The family business was deep in debt. He was going to lose the estate and the horses. My mother was devastated; she lives for those horses. I couldn't stand around and do nothing. I had to help but I wasn't financially sound enough to bail them out. Ava's father is a Greek shipping magnet. He agreed to pay my family's creditors if I married his daughter who was pregnant from a very influential married man. It would be a symbiotic agreement. Ava's family would be spared embarrassment and legal implications if her suitor's wife found out who her baby's real father was. It seemed like the only option at the time. We never consummated the marriage. I swear to God Jesse, I never touched her." Jesse could hear the desperation in his voice. "You have to believe me Jesse; I never meant to hurt you."

"If you never meant to hurt me, then why did you keep your marriage a secret?" asked Jesse. "I had taken over managing my family's business and had already repaid Ava's father the last amount of money he had loaned us. I had already filed for divorce when I met you. You had nothing to do with me wanting to divorce Ava. It would have happened eventually. The marriage was a sham Jesse."

"You haven't answered my question Joshua. Why didn't you just tell me the truth?"

"Because Ava was contesting the divorce and was claiming half of everything. I couldn't let her get her greedy little fingers on *Sonder Moeite*. I have a responsibility to all my shareholders."

"Oh my goodness!" Jesse had an epiphany. "What?"

"That's why you were so suspicious of me being a journalist."

"Yes, I couldn't trust anyone. I've had very negative experiences with journalists in the past. I thought you were like the rest of them. I was wrong. I'm sorry," Josh admitted honestly. "I was so afraid that I would lose *Sonder Moeite* and you." "What do you mean, 'and me'?" asked Jesse confused. "I have loved you from the moment I set eyes on you, Jesse Kearns. The way you walked, the way you smelled, the way you laughed, the way you tilt your head ever so slightly to one side, everything about you has turned my whole world upside down. These last two months have been a living hell for me."

"You've been living in hell for two months but you couldn't pick up the phone to ask me if I was alright?" retorted Jesse. "I knew that it would only be appropriate for me to contact you once the divorce was finalized and it was finalized last week."

"Oh," responded Jesse not knowing exactly what to say. "So do you get to keep *Sonder Moeite*?" she asked feeling stupid about her question. "Only if you'll come and live with me," stated Josh emphatically. "I don't understand…" replied Jesse. "I came here for three reasons Jesse. Firstly to explain what happened and secondly to say I'm sorry and ask your forgiveness. I am truly sorry. Please will you forgive me?" he pleaded. What was she supposed to do? Her heart was as soft as butter. Forgiveness came very easily to Jesse. It was in her nature. She inherited it from her mother. "Yes, I forgive you Joshua and I completely understand," she affirmed. "In that case…" he went down on one knee and pulled something out of his pocket. "Jesse Kearns you are the love of my life, will you marry me?" Staring back at her in a little black velvet encased box was a platinum ring with a tanzanite stone encrusted with sparkling diamonds. Jesse looked at Josh; the troubled look he had worn so often was replaced with unmistakable love. Her eyes filled with tears as she closed them. 'Lord, please don't let this be just my imagination', she thought earnestly. She opened her eyes again and the sparkling stone stared back at her. This was real. "Yes Joshua, I will marry you." Josh slipped the ring on her finger and took her face in his strong hands. He looked deep into her eyes and asked, "Are you sure Jesse? This is it. There will be no divorce. I will never grant you one so you need to be one hundred percent sure."

"Joshua Bolton, I want to have children with you and grow old with you and live happily at *Sonder Moeite*." He leaned forward and kissed her tenderly. Her lips quavered. She had waited so long just to see him, she was afraid that she would wake up and it would all be just a dream.

Josh got up and pulled Jesse to her feet. He pulled her close into his warm hard body and wrapped his arms around her. "You have no idea how much I have missed you. I thought I was going mad with longing for you. Not knowing if you were alright drove me insane," he admitted candidly. "I really thought that you were one of those men who were just out to have a good time with me. I couldn't believe that you would conceal a marriage that well."

"Believe me Jesse; I hated myself for doing that. For so long I wanted to tell you that I was married and the circumstances surrounding the marriage," added Josh. "In fact I nearly told you so many times but I kept worrying that it would be in the news or that you'd disappear out of my life forever. I thought that if I held out for as long as possible I could let you know after the divorce then you wouldn't think it necessary to leave me," he added remorsefully. "You are really full of yourself, you know that?" retorted Jesse. "No, not full of myself, just very sure of certain things, my love," he smiled mockingly. When Jesse saw his unmistakable dimple again, all was truly forgiven.

"I'm really tired," announced Josh wearily. "We could go and lie down," suggested Jesse uncertainly. She wasn't sure if she was exactly comfortable with Joshua Bolton lying in her bed. Would he not think she was easy? Perhaps he was feigning tiredness just to sleep with her. He noticed her hesitation and scooped her up in his arms. "Joshua! What are you doing?" She was helpless against his strong arms. No amount of struggling was going to make him put her down so she just decided to nestle in his arms. Josh carried Jesse into the bedroom and laid her down gently. He kicked his shoes off and lay beside her pulling her into his arms. The two lovebirds lay quietly in each other's arms savouring the moment. Josh couldn't believe that things had worked out so well. He had been terrified that Jesse would meet someone else in his absence. He didn't want to admit to himself that he was jealous of the man that Jesse had danced with at the nightclub earlier. He thought he was her boyfriend and was planning to punch him if things got out of control. Josh sighed because he was glad he hadn't made a fool of himself that night. Jesse definitely would not have forgiven him and maybe he would have lost her forever.

Jesse lay peacefully for a while and then asked curiously, "Josh, how did you know I was at the club?" "I followed you," he responded nonchalantly. "You did not!" she playfully hit his arm with her fist. "I did too," he laughingly defended himself. "Josh, how did you manage to save your parents estate?" "Well, firstly I brought in an external auditor to see where most of the expenses were going. I did a needs analysis on income, loss, business and living expenditure. That way I could see where my father was not managing the business effectively. I also introduced a tourism aspect to the business, where tours would be conducted on horseback over the moors. The concept grew very slowly but later became more and more popular. So now, we have tours in addition to the show jumping and horse riding training. I can guarantee you my father was not happy with me at all."

"Why? You were only trying to help," said Jesse. "Yes, but he saw it as me interfering and trying to show him up as incompetent, which I don't think he is. He simply made some bad decisions that set the ball rolling towards bankruptcy." "But I'm sure he was happy with your decisions because he got to keep the estate," maintained Jesse. "Well, our relationship was quite strained for some time. In fact, I had to sell two of my properties, one in Spain and the other in Scotland but it still couldn't cover the costs, that's why Ava's father stepped in and offered to bail him out." Jesse shuddered at the mention of Ava's name. All she could remember was that woman's shrill mocking laughter. "How did you manage to divorce Ava without having to sell *Sonder Moeite*?" continued Jesse. "It was tough Jesse, but I hired a very good lawyer and I was determined to keep *Sonder Moeite*. The marriage was never consummated and that made it easier for me. Do you know that she claimed her child was mine?" "No way, Josh!" "Yes, I had to go for blood tests that prove paternity and when they came back negative she was on the war path." "So where is Ava now?"

"Somewhere in London, I guess."

"Well I suppose she was a desperate woman and desperate times call for desperate measures. Sometimes we find ourselves in really bad situations and we try to survive by all means possible. I suppose its just human nature," sighed Jesse thoughtfully. It was so like her thought Josh, to try and look for the best in people no matter what their circumstances. Josh felt very comforted by Jesse's presence and he knew instinctively that she would support him through good and bad times. He had really chosen a good woman this time.

They spoke deep into the night planning their future together until they both fell sound asleep. Jesse dreamed that she was walking up a long driveway with large Jacaranda trees on either side. It was autumn and the leaves had all turned brown and orange. The purple flowers had turned to lilac and then dried out and died. The driveway was full of dead leaves and flowers that crunched under her feet as she walked up towards the house. It was already dusk and she could see the glow of warm yellow lights through the windows. As she approached the front steps of the house, the door opened and a tall man came out to greet her. He looked down at her, his hazel eyes sparkling. He smiled at her and she could see a wicked little dimple dancing at the corner of his mouth. She knew that she had come home; that everything would be all right and that her safety and happiness was sealed in the love of this man. He took her hand in his and walked into the house, shutting the door tightly behind him. Jesse woke up the next morning feeling rested and completely at peace with herself.

Chapter 12

Jesse awoke early the following morning and slid quietly out of bed so as not to awaken Josh. She dressed in her short pink negligee and stood in front of the stove making breakfast. She was never one for wearing dressing gowns, except when she was not in her own home. They seemed to stifle her. The scrambled eggs and toast were already made and Jesse was busy frying the last pancake. Today she seemed to have a raving appetite. Josh walked into the kitchen watching her long curly hair trailing past her waistline. Her tanned legs glistened and her bare feet looked so child like. He walked over to her and put his arms around her, while his sensual thoughts flooded to the foreground of his mind. Her hair smelled like fresh shampoo, her skin was smooth and silky soft. "This is what I like to see, my woman bare foot behind the stove," he teased her laughingly. "Go and make the coffee and butter the toast please! She ordered him. "Gee wiz, I feel henpecked already," he answered as he ducked from her hand that was waving the egg lifter towards his head.

They sat down to breakfast and Josh pulled Jesse onto his lap. They ate together. She feeding him bits of toast and he tenderly feeding her honey dripped pancake bites. He kissed the corners of her mouth and sucked the honey from her soft warm lips. "This was the best breakfast I've ever had," he moaned burying his head into her neck, caressing her heaving breast. Jesse tilted her head back slightly and moaned passionately. Josh picked her up and carried Jesse to the bedroom. Their lovemaking lasted a long time. He savoured every bit of her lithe supple body. He was in no hurry and was making up for lost time. She moaned his name softly as he entered her gently. Her body was warm and inviting. Josh made Jesse feel like a woman a thousand times over. Just as she thought she was about to reach her peak he would withdraw and find another spot on her body with his delicate touch. She had no idea that a man could give a woman this much pleasure. She felt completely relaxed knowing that he knew

92

her body so well already. He knew what turned her on. With Josh, she didn't have to pretend or fake anything. They finally both reached the height of their pleasure and lay panting in each other's arms. It had been a long time since he had felt this relaxed. With Jesse, he could let his guard down. Unlike with Ava, he was always waiting for the knife to penetrate his back. Josh looked deep into her eyes. A tear formed and he whispered ardently, "Jesse Kearns I love you with all my heart." She smiled back at him knowing exactly what he meant. Her heart felt like exploding too. The couple fell asleep in each other's arms once again. Their love was sealed, and their souls united.

The next day they decided to make plans for their future together. "I want you to meet my family," he declared. "What if they don't like me," she asked nervously. "What's not to like," he stated firmly. "In any case it's my job to like you not theirs." He noticed her worried eyes like those of a deer caught in oncoming headlights. "Don't worry my love everything will be fine." "Well, in that case you'll have to meet my extended family as well. We'll have one big party so you can meet everyone at the same time. "Good! After the party, we'll fly to England and meet the Bolton clan and then we can start the wedding preparations. How does that sound to you my love?" "Perfect, Josh, I can't wait," squealed Jesse excitedly. She thought of all the plans she would have to make; the party invitations, the food, the venue, the décor. Then she would have to buy a few new outfits to fly to England. Oh boy! She still had to think about the wedding preparations. She'd get her dear friend Amanda to help with the planning.

Jesse brought pen and paper to draw up a list of all the family and friends she should invite to her 'introduce Joshua to the family' party. As the length of the list started increasing, she said worriedly to Joshua, "Where will we fit all these people? My flat is too small!" "Don't worry love; we'll just hire a hotel restaurant. That way you won't have to worry about the catering and we can just mingle." Josh was so tactful and such a gentleman, in the way that he suggested a hotel restaurant. He knew that Jesse couldn't afford to entertain so many people and spending money to make his future wife happy gave him enormous pleasure. "In any case I'm going to need you close by my side all night."

"Why?" mocked Jesse, laughingly, "Is the tough Joshua Bolton afraid of my family.

"You do know that I have to create a good impression and I won't be able to do that if I can't remember all their names. You'll be whispering their names in my ear all night," he mused with a glint in his eye. "Yeh right! And my family will think we are whispering sweet nothings to each other all night," she laughed. Joshua was right as usual. He had thought of the planning and foresaw how complicated the evening would become had they had to make all the arrangements themselves. On the other hand, he could afford to splash out on this function. Money had never been an issue with Joshua Bolton, perhaps because he had more than enough of it. Jesse liked the fact that he never bragged about his wealth and never threw money about. Few people knew exactly how much he was in fact worth. They both decided to make the function as informal as possible. Joshua made the hotel restaurant arrangements. Jesse got on the phone and telephoned all those on her list, inviting them to meet her fiancé. She also got her dear friend Amanda to help decorate the restaurant. Jesse knew that she wanted to depict her first impression of Robertson. And clearly, the Jacaranda lined streets were what fore mostly stood out in her mind. This was the vision she wanted to capture in the restaurant. So she chose purple and lilac with silver. Amanda was very artistic and she placed white tablecloths with purple overlays and lilac serviettes tied with silver ribbons. There were bouquets with lilac and white flowers on the tables. When she had finished she agreed that it did look very good.

94

It was Friday, the day of the party, where Joshua was going to meet Jesse's family. There was a lot of excitement in the air. The telephone rang nonstop. Family members wanted to know what they should wear or what they should bring to the party. In Jesse's family, it was a tradition, that at family gatherings, each member brought their favourite dish. This gesture was always welcome as it made lighter work for the hosts. Jesse's family was not very well off or influential but they were extremely down to earth and warmhearted. Jesse thanked them for their concern but reminded them that the hotel would do all the catering and that they should simply come and enjoy themselves. Jesse reminded Joshua that it was considered good manners to ask his future in-laws for permission to marry their daughter as well as for their blessing. "Don't worry," he assured her, "I've already practiced my speech in front of the mirror. "'It is with great honor Ms Kearns snr. that I, Joshua Bolton, am asking for the hand of your daughter,'" he bowed with one hand behind his back. "That's good! Laugh and play the fool. I'd like to see who is going to lose their nerve tonight when they meet my mother." Josh was secretly a bit nervous about meeting her folks. He was glad that he didn't have to ask her father for her hand in marriage. However, he wanted to create a good impression but wasn't sure how her family would respond to him especially because of the legacy that the British had left behind in South Africa and because of the legacy Jesse's father had also left behind. He hoped that they didn't think that all British men were the same.

The couple left Jesse's flat just after seven o'clock. It was a warm balmy evening with many twinkling stars in the evening sky, winking at them as if promising some potential undisclosed delights for the evening ahead. Jesse wore a white cotton wrap blouse and blue denim jeans with leopard skin peep toe high-heeled shoes. Her hair swung disobediently over her shoulders down to her waist. Joshua had blue denim jeans on and an expensive light tan leather jacket. They looked so happy as he held her hand while he led her to his sports car. He opened the door for her and she slid comfortably into her familiar seat. She looked on admiringly as he started the engine. Jesse found enormous comfort in this man's presence.

When they arrived at the hotel, the manager escorted the couple to the main restaurant. Everybody was already there. Josh and Jesse could hear lots of chatter and music coming from behind the large closed door. As the manager opened the door, a hush fell on the room. Everyone just stared. South Africans inadvertently always think in terms of race – a result of the legacy of *apartheid* - and perhaps they were expecting a person of the same race group. Josh held Jesse's hand a little tighter and raised his right hand to the crowd. "Good evening and welcome," he said in his deep English accented voice. Everyone started clapping for the happy couple and the ice was immediately broken. Jesse was relieved but Josh was even more relieved. The chatter and the music continued once more. She looked around the room in search of her mother. Suddenly ahead of them, the room started clearing and a very exotic looking woman walked towards them. She had Jesse's eyes, thought Josh or rather Jesse had her eyes. They were large, almond shaped and very smoky but the fine lines underneath her eyes spoke of her years of struggle and wisdom. She smiled warmly as she approached them holding out both her hands. Jesse's mother was slightly shorter than her daughter was. Her complexion was more copper than bronze and her build was still athletic. "Mama, I've missed you." "My baby, how are you sweetheart?" she asked. They hugged for a while. "I'm so glad you came," breathed Jesse excitedly. "How could I miss my only child's engagement party?" she uttered holding Jesse's face in her hands. "It's not an engagement party, Mama!" "It is to me," she voiced her opinion strongly. Josh witnessed the close bond they had and he felt slightly jealous. Both women turned to him simultaneously as if reading his thoughts. "Mama, this is Joshua Bolton. Josh, please meet my mother Rebecca Kearns." Josh extended his hand but

96

Rebecca ignored it and stepped forward embracing her future son in law. He was taken by complete surprise; and hugged her in return. This show of affection from a stranger was all so new to him. "Joshua, we need to talk," she ordered. "Yes M'am," he obliged. Rebecca Kearns hooked her hand into Josh's bent elbow and steered him to a quiet part of the room. Josh seemed like putty in her hands. Jesse secretly hoped her mother would grill him. He had played the fool earlier, well now it was his turn. Jesse mingled with some of her aunts and cousins. There were many questions thrown at her. "When will the wedding take place?" "Where would she live?" "How many children was she planning to have?" "What would happen to her job if she moved to England or *Sonder Moeite?*" "Was she going to be a stay-at-home mom or a career woman?" Jesse laughed out aloud. She had not even thought through these questions, let alone the answers. She assured her family that she would take one day at a time and discuss all these questions in detail with her future husband, before she made any rash decisions One thing she did know however, was that she still wanted to maintain her independence.

When Josh returned to her side, he was beaming from ear to ear. "Oh, I take it that went very well," mocked Jesse. He pulled her close to him and kissed her. Looking deep into her eyes he said, "Your mother is the best mother in law any guy could hope to have. She has given her blessing and her warning that if I don't look after you properly, I'll have her to answer to. She wants us to have the wedding in South Africa and I agreed with her." Jesse jumped up and threw her arms around his neck. Everything was working out perfectly.

They mingled for the rest of the evening. Jesse introduced Josh to her aunts, uncles and cousins. Josh was completely blown away by how friendly, warm and welcoming everybody was towards him. The evening progressed very smoothly. The food was delicious. The hotel staff had included all Jesse's favourite food, a range of salads, snoek fish grilled in garlic butter, mutton breyani (meat and rice dish), curry and roti, grilled chickens with an assortment of vegetables and rolls. The desserts were scrumptious. There were koeksisters, malva pudding, sago pudding, bread pudding, fruit salad and ice cream, milk tarts, chocolate and carrot cakes. Josh had insisted that all her needs be met, in terms of the food. Jesse felt a little guilty. "What about your favourite foods Joshua?" she insisted. "Darling, we cannot serve the guests bangers and mash or cucumber sandwiches now can we?" he laughed. "I'm afraid we British don't have much of a choice when it comes to food. I am used to South African food now and I have my favourites among yours as well," he assured her.

The band started playing traditional Cape Town ballroom music. Josh took Jesse onto the dance floor as the guests cleared a space for them. The waltz was so romantic as he took her from one corner to the next, hovering here and there, twisting their bodies in time with the music. Jesse could feel his hard body pressed against her. They danced as one. Josh took her into the fishtail and glided out again maneuvering his partner expertly across the floor. It was so beautiful to watch and Jesse could see the admiration in everyone's eyes. As the music tapered to an end, the guests were already clapping and cheering for them. Then in true Cape Town style, everyone was on the floor as the beat of the music increased. The festivities lasted until late into the night. Joshua was officially part of the family now. He was treated as though he had been present for years like an old friend who had simply gone away for a while. This acceptance of him really warmed his heart and he knew he had made a good choice in a future wife because his father had always warned him that when you marry, you don't only marry your partner but the whole family. Jesse came from a good family and Josh could see this by the way that they conducted themselves.

The couple returned to Jesse's flat late that night. It was an evening that neither of them would forget in a long time. They were both exhausted but chatted in bed for some time. "I must admit I really didn't know what to expect but I had a very warm welcome from your folks," Josh said relieved. "My poor darling, you thought you were going to the slaughter house," Jesse laughed cuddling closer to him in the large bed. "I wouldn't laugh if I were you," he warned, "Your turn is still coming." "As long as you're with me, I know I'll be fine," she boasted smilingly. They lay in each other's arms. There was nothing more that could satisfy them; they already had everything – each other.

Soon Josh fell sound asleep but Jesse lay awake for a long time, Josh's words ringing in her ears. *'Your time is still coming'.* She wondered if she was not being too hasty about Josh and especially meeting his parents. A little voice in her head kept nagging her to re-evaluate her situation. Her mother had always told her that the best predictor of future behaviour was past behaviour. Josh had not behaved very well in the past. He had not communicated his feelings for her nor his dilemma with Ava. His father may be eternally grateful to Ava's family for helping them in a time when they nearly lost everything. And Ava was very beautiful, in a classic kind of way. Deep in her heart, she knew that she was taking a huge risk by allowing herself to be drawn into Josh's world and his heart. Jesse knew that in order to have a successful relationship, communication was the key. It concerned her that she still had to contend with Josh's family as well – she had no money or influential connections – unlike Ava. She could not offer Josh or his family what Ava could offer. All she had to offer was her heart. The fact that his father was British was also another hurdle she had to jump. She hadn't even asked Josh if he had told his father that she was bi-racial. So now, she would have to work doubly hard to win their trust and their respect. Jesse tossed and turned until eventually she fell asleep.

Chapter 13

The next morning Josh had to make his way back to *Sonder Moeite*. He turned to look at Jesse. She looked so peaceful and beautiful with her long dark lashes draped over her smoky almond eyes. Her breathing was regular and Josh simply lay there admiring her. When she awoke, she found Josh staring at her. She smiled, stretched and slipped her arms around his neck. He pulled her up onto him and she could already feel his manhood hardening beneath her. He traced the outline of her body with his fingers. Her curves were long and deep. Finally, in one sweeping movement he turned Jesse onto her back and mounted her. He looked deep into her eyes without saying a word. They both knew what they wanted. His hand parted her warm thighs and found her delicious secret parts. Stroking her precious jewel with his shaft, he slowly went inside her. She was hot and moist. He went searching for something he knew was there but had to explore deeper and deeper to find it. She moaned his name aloud. "Oh Joshua!" it made him wild. She sent shivers down his spine. He would go to the ends of the earth to satisfy this woman. He kissed her breasts until they were as firm as melons. Finally, they were spent. Josh didn't want to release Jesse. He wished their bodies were bound together forever. "C'mon Josh," she kissed his neck, "you know I have to go to work." He rolled off her reluctantly. "You'll have to make up to me when you come next weekend.

This was to be their routine every weekend, until Jesse had worked out her notice period with the Cape Town Post. A long distance relationship was not so bad. In fact, it was rather exciting. She waited in anticipation for his call every evening. Most days he would surprise her with a phone call at an odd hour, flowers would arrive with a cryptic note or a small present would be couriered to her desk. It was a very exciting period in Jesse's life and it gave them both an opportunity to get to know each other a little better.

100

When Jesse found herself at *Sonder Moeite* on weekends Beth would dote on her excitedly because she was very keen to have another woman in the house again. "This house needs a womanly touch Miss Jesse," she'd say. When Josh was in the fields supervising the workers, Jesse and Beth would look through magazines and discuss different décor styles and colours for the new look of *Sonder Moeite*. Jesse didn't want to get an interior designer to redecorate her future home. She wanted to do it herself so that she could keep busy but also more importantly so that she could add her own taste to her new home, especially after the whole Ava situation.

Jesse's notice period at the Cape Town Post was almost over. "If ever you need a job here again Jesse, please don't hesitate to come back. There will always be a home here for you," confirmed Mitch caringly. "That's very kind of you Mitch. I will never forget you." Mitch felt that Jesse leaving the journalism field would be a great loss to the media world. As a last attempt to tempt her he added, "You don't have to leave journalism entirely Jesse. You could become a freelance journalist and work wherever you are in the world." "That is a brilliant idea Mitch. I will definitely consider it because I'll still want to maintain some semblance of independence," she confirmed.

The very weekend after her notice period was over and she had left the Cape Town Post, Jesse went into a frenzy of shopping for her trip to London. She purchased some stylish outfits and Josh went with her to most of her dress fittings. He would give her his honest critical opinion as she modeled in front of him. Josh was not afraid to spend money on his bride to be. He wanted her to have the best because he felt that she deserved the best. She felt very sexy and desirable in front of him.

Finally their departure date arrived. As they seated themselves in the jumbo jet-waiting to take off, Jesse leaned her head against Josh's broad shoulder and said, "I was so excited to meet your family, now I'm feeling a wave of apprehension and nerves." "What are you worried about? They're just people my love, with hopes, dreams, desires and flaws like any other family. You'll be fine," he consoled her. "Have you even told your parents that I'm bi-racial?" asked Jesse concerned. "Will you stop it! You are the woman I love and besides my mother is almost your complexion," he added trying to diffuse her anxiety. "What if they compare me to Ava?" There she finally said that woman's name aloud. From the beginning that name had been the root of all her troubles with Joshua. Josh stiffened slightly and she detected his jaw pulsating at one corner. He turned and looking straight at her, he cupped her pretty face in his large strong hands and gently but sternly stated. "Jesse, my darling, I never want to hear that woman's name again. She is out of my life, thank God! Now it is our time, let's not waste it on someone so insignificant please." There was finality in his voice and a hardness that she had never detected before. "I'm sorry Josh, that was very insensitive of me," she apologized. He squeezed her hand and put his arm around her. They were a united front against the world and nothing would break them apart, least of all his past.

The aeroplane took off smoothly and before long, they were airborne. Jesse turned to look out of the window and she could see the rooftops of houses getting smaller and smaller. The distance between her and her native land became wider and wider. Jesse began to panic. Something inside of her told her to let go. She realized that she was hanging onto what she was accustomed to, what was familiar to her. Then she said to herself, "Jesse, you're entering a new life with new and adventurous possibilities." There and then she decided to let go of the old and embrace this new adventure with this strong man she had fallen so hopelessly in love with.

Soon Jesse began to feel drowsy. Her eyes grew heavy and her head leaned lightly on Josh's shoulder. He looked over at her and smiled.

Jesse was soon sound asleep. Her breathing became regular and she dreamt that she was walking along a beach. The water was warm and inviting but something told her not to go far into the water. She walked holding her skirt in her hands. Suddenly a huge wave washed over her, pulling her to the ground and dragging her into the sea. She screamed but no sound came from her lips. She struggled to breathe and panic set in. As she lashed out at the sea, a hand grabbed hers and pulled her to shore. When she was finally able to catch her breath, she looked up at the stranger's face and realized that it was Joshua. His expression was cold. Jesse wanted to thank him for helping her but he seemed to look right through her. Every ounce of her being wanted to call out to him and say, '*Joshua, it's me Jesse, the woman you love.*' But she could not find her voice; her being seemed to fail her. The kindness she had come to know was replaced by brutality. As she opened her mouth, he simply walked away. "*Wait!*" she shouted, but he had already disappeared. What had happened to her Joshua? Who was this stranger? Jesse ran in the direction in which the 'stranger' had disappeared, "*Wait!*" she called again, but all she could see were the crashing waves on the beach. Jesse woke up startled. "Are you alright, love?" Josh asked concerned. "I had the strangest dream," she said trying to shake herself out of this weird unconscious experience. It was hard to believe that the man she had fallen so hopelessly in love with could be so cold and callous. The dream deeply disturbed Jesse but she didn't want Josh to know what her thoughts were. Not now, especially since she was going to meet his family. "Was I asleep long," she asked Josh guiltily. "No, but you're just in time for dinner. The catering cart is on its way down the aisle." Jesse looked out of the window into the clouds. 'Who was that 'stranger' in my dream?' thought Jesse. Why had Josh forsaken her like that? Was there another side to him that he had not yet revealed to her? This red flag flew high in Jesse mind.

The flight was long and tiresome. They stopped in Nigeria to refuel sometime during the night. Whenever she had an opportunity, she would get up and walk up and down the aisle to stretch her legs and get the blood circulating in her cramped body. Josh didn't seem perturbed at all with the long flight. He was clearly used to this, having traveled regularly between London and Cape Town. He kept busy on his laptop with the accounting of the farm as well as productivity plans for the next six months.

Suddenly the flight captain announced their descent into Heathrow airport. Jesse was filled with angst, looking to Josh for assurance. He pulled her close to him and kissed her temple. "Don't worry; we're only meeting my family tomorrow. I would never be so cruel to you after such a long flight," he coaxed her. "I've booked us into a hotel for the night and we can travel to Cornwall in the morning. Jesse breathed a sigh of relief. She had very little strength left, to be meeting people.

Finally, they disembarked and Jesse's feet touched British soil for the second time in her life. A bus took them to customs and the baggage carousel at the airport terminal. There were hundreds of people everywhere. Jesse could hear many different languages spoken. Some people looked lost, others were searching for their luggage and still others were hurrying to meet their loved ones. Once Josh located their luggage, they went to the car rental office and he hired a car. Of course, it had to be a German car, Josh believed in German engineering and luxury. He cruised to their hotel, knowing exactly which shortcuts and side roads to take in order to avoid most of the traffic. Jesse was in awe of the beautiful buildings and she could recognize some of the places from her last trip to London.

Once they had checked in to their hotel, which looked like an old English cottage, Jesse unpacked a few things while Josh ran her a hot bubble bath. He could see how exhausted she looked and he pitied her for putting her through such a long trip. Jesse undressed and climbed into the inviting bubbles. She lay there soaking away while Josh was in the shower next door. 'This feels so good,' she thought. Jesse drifted away quietly and images of the dream she had had on the aeroplane came filtering back to her. Should she tell Josh about the dream? Perhaps it was only a silly dream. Jesse decided not to tell Josh but to wait and see what would happen in Cornwall.

When Jesse came out of the bathroom towel draped around her, Josh was already asleep on the bed with only a towel draped around his waist. Jesse took the opportunity to admire his tanned body. Muscles gleamed in the soft light of the bedside lamp. His chest heaved slightly as the dark hair seemed to tumble in confusion around his pectoral muscles. Jesse got into bed next to Josh and he unconsciously pulled her closer towards him. She felt safe as she nestled in his strong arm. Soon exhaustion took over and she too fell fast asleep.

When she awoke the next morning Josh was on the telephone ordering room service breakfast. He smiled at her as she stretched her long legs lazily. By the time he had put the telephone down she was in the shower. Jesse washed away all the tiredness and emerged refreshed. A small towel draped her petite body with her hair toweled in a turban. She dressed in jeans and a cotton top. Jesse blow-dried her hair quickly and applied a small amount of silicone gel to her hair so the curls would stay in place. As she reached for her comb, Josh already had it in his hand. "Allow me," he stated, combing her hair with such gentleness and appreciation of her beauty. Her long hair seemed to go on and on down her back. "I never want you to cut your hair, it's so beautiful," he added tenderly. "I'll cut it when I turn fifty. You surely don't want a woman with long grey hair now do you?" she mocked. "Long grey hair in a bun on the top of your head. That will do it for me," he nodded laughing. Jesse laughed too but her heart was apprehensive. Just then, there was a knock at the door.

"Room service," called a waiter. A decent breakfast was what they both needed.

Chapter 14

The drive to Cornwall from London was long but oh so very picturesque. They drove through many little villages and large towns. It was green everywhere, with rambling creepers interlaced with roses and ivy. The landscape was beautiful. One green hill seemed to roll into another. Occasionally they would pass herds of sheep herded by a shepherd. After about two and a half hours of driving, they had reached Bodmin in Cornwall. They continued past the market and beyond. Josh gave the town a wide birth, knowing that he would show the town to Jesse later that week. He pointed out Bodmin moor to Jesse and told her that this was where he and his brother Nico often rode their horses among the rough hills. About ten kilometers out of town, he took a left turn where a signpost read BOLTON EQUESTRIAN ESTATE. They reached high steel gates with horse emblems on either side. The gates looked strangely familiar. Jesse could see where Josh had gotten the idea from at the *Sonder Moeite* farm. A caretaker opened the gates and chattered excitedly, "Welcome home, Mr Bolton, good to see you sir," he said - with the yellowiest teeth Jesse had ever seen. He peered at her inquisitively as he waved at the moving vehicle. The perimeter of the property was metered in chestnut trees with a short hedge on the inside boundary that seemed to go on for miles. As Josh drove up the lane, there were fields on either side and Jesse could see horses grazing peacefully. On a farther hill, she could see a group of people galloping on horses. They seemed to be flying in the wind. Jesse could not speak. All she could do was take in all this beauty and wealth. She had no idea that Josh's family was this wealthy. He had never given her any indication of the extent of their wealth.

Josh drove up a long winding gravel driveway. They reached the front of the house and parked under a pillared patio. Josh looked at Jesse and stated excitedly, "We're home!" But home was not a house. It was a mansion. It seemed to be the size of ten normal houses put together. A reddish brown brick building; this appeared to be Georgian in structure but had had an extreme makeover. It was large but very modern looking. "You live here?" asked Jesse bewildered. "Yep! Don't worry my love, my family are just ordinary people," he encouraged. As they drove up to the front steps, two maids came running towards them. "Welcome home, Mr Bolton. We trust you had a pleasant trip sir?" "Thank you Susan. Please meet my fiancée, Jesse Kearns. I am entrusting Jesse's care in your capable hands Susan," he commanded. Susan and the other maid looked at Jesse admiringly and took their bags. Josh took Jesse's hand firmly in his and guided her up the grey marbled steps towards the stylish entrance.

As they entered the large marbled hallway, a very tall Italian looking woman came gliding down the large winding staircase. She had thick jet-black hair, large hazel eyes, a beautiful aquiline nose and a wide red mouth. She looked like an opera singer. Now Jesse understood where Josh got his good looks from. The woman stopped briefly to look at the new arrivals, unsure of who they might be. When she spotted Josh, her entire face lit up. "Oh darling! You're home!" she exclaimed excitedly. She raced down the violet-carpeted stairs and threw her arms around her son speaking Italian very rapidly and stepping back to look at him and pointing her finger at him while a torrid of words escaped her red mouth. She hugged him again. Josh seemed like plasticine in her hands. "Mama, I am well and I'm here now so please don't scold me," he laughed. Josh turned to introduce his future bride to his mother. Mrs Bolton held out both hands and exclaimed, "*Bellissima bella!*" She took Jesse's hand and twirled her around. She did this so that she could get a better look at the woman who was to wed her son. Then nodded, pleased and excited. "I am very pleased to meet you Jesse dear and you are most welcome!" she exclaimed in her Italian accent. Mrs Bolton put her arm around Jesse and led her upstairs. Josh was extremely relieved to say the least. He was secretly worried because his mother had very high standards and she had been vehemently opposed to his marriage with Ava. Now he had to jump the next hurdle. His father was not easy to please either and was always biased against non-British people even though he had married an Italian woman himself. Josh always thought that his father applied double standards when it came to others.

Shortly after they had settled into their respective rooms and freshened up, Josh decided to take Jesse on a tour of the house. The building was extremely large and filled with history. There were many family portraits in the hallways and passages. Jesse thought that some of the quarters were rather dark and staid. She visualized herself doing an extreme makeover for some of the rooms. She'd put long bright taffeta and organza drapes on the large windows or perhaps turn some of the rooms into theme rooms, like Arabian or Victorian rooms. Jesse was having a wonderful time playing imaginary games when Josh opened another door, which turned out to be the nursery. Jesse was enthralled. There was a wooden rocking horse near the window and chests with toys. On one side of the wall loomed a large bed. On the opposite side of the bed stood a playpen filled with farm animal toys. It was a lovely powder blue room, any child's dream habitat. The wall opposite the large bay windows had a mural of a forest and flowers painted on it; a version of Hansel and Gretel making their way home by following some breadcrumbs on their footpath through the forest. The sun shone through the bay windows. The sunlight was captured through the mural treetops, filtering down onto the beautiful painted wallflowers making it look so real. "So, what do you think?" asked Josh curiously. "Oh, it's beautiful Josh! You must've had so much fun playing here," she added. Josh walked slowly towards Jesse, his mouth warming and the hazel dots in his eyes appearing to dance around wickedly. He pulled Jesse towards him and planted his mouth on hers, kissing her passionately. "So how many bambinos do you think we should have?" he asked moaning in the crook of her neck. "Only two!" she stated emphatically. "Only two?" he faked a hurt look on his face. "I certainly hope you're not going to deprive me in the bedroom, Ms Kearns," mocked Josh moving Jesse towards the bed. "What are you doing? This is your parent's house. Have some respect!" hissed Jesse straightening out her blouse and neatening her hair. Josh laughed and took her hand leading her out of the nursery. "Let's go and see if my father has arrived yet.

Coming down the long passage, they heard voices in the library. Josh opened the heavy door to a room filled with books from floor to wall. There was a large reading table in the centre of the room and two large picture windows with a large mosaic stone fireplace between them at the far end of the room. Above the mosaic, stone fireplace hung an imposing oil painting of the cliffs and sea of Cornwall. The view from the picture windows showed the greenest meadows Jesse had ever seen. Two leather chairs were turned towards the fireplace and an exquisite green brocade sofa with cushions stood opposite the fireplace. It was a lived in room. An elderly man with a weather beaten face sat reading a newspaper. He looked up when he saw Josh. A wide smile spread across his face when he recognized his eldest son but suddenly something in his expression froze when he saw Jesse. She noticed it immediately. Josh and his father shook hands and patted each other on the back. "You look well, son. South Africa seems to have been good to you." "Very good indeed, father," he added turning to Jesse. "Please meet my future bride, Jesse Kearns." He shook Jesse's hand staring at her. "You look strangely familiar," he said trying to place her face. Josh's father wasn't rude but he didn't seem particularly friendly either. Jesse couldn't help but think that he did not approve of her marrying his son. "I thought I heard voices before we entered the library, father?" "Just got off the phone with Bill," informed the older man. "How is the old goat?" enquired Josh. Just then, Josh's mother came in trailed by two maids carrying tea and scones. Tea commenced with light-hearted chatter. Josh's mother wanted to know all about *Sonder Moeite* and his father enquired about the country's economy as well as Josh's network of

110

business acquaintances. During the entire conversation, Josh's father's eyes kept reverting to Jesse as if he was desperately trying to figure out where he had met her or it could be that he was judging her person. Perhaps, Jesse thought, he was wondering if a brown-skinned person was as capable as a white skinned person. He tried hard to hide his interest or was it his concern? 'No doubt', Jesse thought,' he would probably have a private conversation with his son to ascertain her credibility.' 'Ah well!' she thought, 'you can't please everybody.' If he did not approve of her, because of her mixed heritage that was his problem. There was absolutely nothing that she could do about her skin tone. And in fact, she was glad of her bronze complexion. It suited her perfectly and added to her exotic exterior. But still, she couldn't forget the way he had stared at her – it had unnerved her. After tea, Jesse excused herself in order to rest a little and to freshen up. She lay on her bed excited yet exhausted. Soon enough, sleep overcame her and she drifted away to another land.

Josh's father was relieved that Jesse had left the room. Now he had an opportunity to grill his son. "She looks terribly familiar, Josh!" "Perhaps you met her in another lifetime," joked Josh. "Nonsense! Her eyebrows, mouth and the shape of her face look familiar. Where is she from? How did you meet her? Do you know what her credentials are?" implored Mr. Bolton snr. "Father, please! You will have an opportunity to get to know her better. She is the best thing that has ever happened to me and I would like you to respect that," added Josh firmly. "I have enormous respect for you, son. You have sacrificed yourself too many times for this family and this time I want to be sure that you are happy," responded the older man. "I am happy, as long as Jesse is at my side." "Well, I think that she is a wonderful choice for a wife," retorted his mother giving her husband a black look. "It's about time this family celebrated something good. Jesse is like a breath of fresh air and we will definitely support you with this marriage, Joshua." His mother gave her husband a look that forced him to agree. "Of course, of course we support you, son. I just

111

wish I knew more about her," he muttered under his breath, always wanting to have the last say.

After tea, Josh and his father strode off to the stables where he was introduced to some new horses. Nico, his younger brother gave him a run down of the financial affairs of the estate since his absence. Nico was two or three centimetres shorter than Josh with a slightly more stocky build. He had light brown hair with the same hazel eyes but he had two dimples, one on either cheek. This gave him a very mischievous countenance. It appeared difficult for him to lie. His dimples would give him away quite easily. Nico was very fond of Josh. Josh had always been his riding partner and he had missed Josh terribly when he had left for South Africa. The two brothers chatted excitedly about the new horses and Nico urged him to go riding with him. "Aw, come on Josh, you have to ride blackbird. He's a powerful horse. He will take you to places you've never been before," encouraged Nico. Josh could not resist a challenge. He was an adrenalin junkie. It was easy for Nico to persuade him to go riding. Both brothers mounted their horses. Josh took immediate control of Blackbird. It seemed as if he had just ridden yesterday. He handled the horse confidently and the two brothers galloped off through the meadows towards Bodmin moor. The mist and the rough tor called out to him – he was hooked once again.

Josh's mother chatted excitedly to her husband. "I can see Josh is truly in love. What a beautiful girl he has chosen!" "Beauty isn't everything, Gina! I can't help worrying about this girl. Why is Josh being so secretive?" he remarked worriedly. "Oh, do you have to be so paranoid, Andrew! He did say you will get to know her better later. Or would you rather put the poor girl under cross examination now?" retorted Mrs Bolton. Mr Bolton snr didn't seem to hear her. Her outburst did not perturb him at all. When his mind had told him a certain thing that was what he would focus on. "We don't know anything about her family, Gina!" he exclaimed. "And neither does she know anything about our family. If I were her I'd run for the hills," retorted his wife raising her voice and throwing her hands up in the air. She spoke a torrid of Italian, partly to her husband and partly to the Lord in order to voice her disdain.

In the meanwhile, Jesse lay sleeping peacefully. She dreamt that she was taking an early morning stroll on the Bolton estate. As she ascended a little hill, she noticed a man coming from the opposite direction. He walked casually towards her. A strange excitement filled her heart. He greeted and continued on his way. Jesse found him strangely familiar. A feeling of peacefulness and protection filled her. It was a feeling she had never felt before. When Jesse woke up, she could still feel a sense of peacefulness and protection. She clung to the feeling, afraid that if she opened her eyes she would lose it. Just then, there was a soft tap on her bedroom door. "Come in," she said sleepily. "Oh, I didn't mean to wake you dear. The boys are out riding. I just came to tell you that dinner will be served in an hour. You might want to freshen up before you come down," she added apologetically. "Thank you Mrs Bolton, I would like to have a shower before I come down," emphasized Jesse. "Okay good. And please call me Gina," she insisted. Jesse smiled uncomfortably as she closed the door behind her. 'Gina!' she said aloud to herself. 'What a pretty name'. Still, how could she call her future mother-in-law by her first name? Jesse's family did not raise her that way. Where she came from, people regarded that as forward and disrespectful. However, she had to remember that she was dealing with a very different culture now.

Jesse had a long invigorating shower. 'Mrs Bolton had been very subtle at reminding her that they dressed for dinner in her home. This must be their culture, very English indeed.' thought Jesse. She got out of the shower and draped a towel around her. Standing there dripping wet she looked around the room and couldn't see her suitcase. 'Oh no!' she thought. 'I didn't bring my suitcase up.' Her brain raced about frantically not knowing what to do. Jesse breathed deeply trying to calm herself down. She walked over to a huge Georgian styled wardrobe and opened it hoping to find a gown or some kind of robe. There in the wardrobe were all her clothes hanging neatly and in order. All her pants were hanging on one rail; her dresses were hanging in order of length and colour – from light to dark. It appeared as though elves had been hard at work. Someone had been very considerate. She could see that whoever did this had taken great pride in their work. Jesse smiled and took down an empire styled dress that flowed to just over her knees. The softly textured royal blue fabric had daintily printed flowers scattered across her chest area. She combed her hair and allowed the tendrils and curls to fall to her waist. Jesse was not really one for lots of makeup but this evening she decided to put on some eyeliner to accentuate her almond smoky eyes. Her eyes looked larger now and more innocent. She put a dash of light mauve lipstick on and pressing her lips together, she smiled into the mirror. 'Hhmm,' she thought, 'that will give Mr Bolton snr something to think about. Jesse's feet climbed into a low healed silver slip-on sandal. She walked towards the bedroom door and turned around to make sure that she had left the room in a tidy state. Jesse then stepped into the long passage. As she closed the door, Susan came out of the next room. "Oh Susan!" she remarked earnestly, "Did you unpack my clothes?" "Yes M'am, I hope that everything is in order?" she asked nervously. "Oh yes of course! I just wanted to thank you for being so thoughtful. It was very kind of you to unpack my things," remarked Jesse appreciatively. "You are most welcome M'am," added Susan. "Please call me Jesse." "Yes M'am," responded Susan once more. Jesse smiled and wondered if Beth would fit into this formal environment. Make no mistake everybody knew their place in this household. At this point Jesse felt glad to have Beth as her future housekeeper. She was glad that she was South African. 'We are just plain, down to earth people," she smiled to herself.

114

Jesse reached the front hallway and was unsure of what to do. The large house was very quiet and Josh was nowhere in sight. She tapped softly on the library door and opened it. Mr Bolton snr looked up and smiled nervously. He invited her to join him next to the dying fire. Now he had an opportunity to ask the questions that were bothering him. "Some sherry?" he asked lifting up a small decanter. "Oh, no thanks," she responded anxiously. Jesse didn't like the taste of alcohol but she also didn't want to appear boorish in front of this sophisticated man. Jesse could hear her grandmother's voice inside her head. *"Just be yourself dear; that is your greatest defense and greatest asset."* Her grandmother was wise and Jesse decided to follow her advice. "I don't drink any alcohol, Mr Bolton," stated Jesse. "Oh, did you have a drinking problem in the past?" he enquired quite brazenly. Jesse smiled because she had an idea where this conversation was going. She could not hold it against him. Perhaps she would have responded similarly had her son been marrying an unknown woman from a foreign country. "Mr Bolton, I just can't stand the taste of alcohol. Alcohol tastes like medicine to me and I will not force myself to acquire a taste for it," she smiled. She thought that old Bolton could take that bit of information which ever way he wanted. He looked oddly at his own glass as if trying to remember when it was that he had learned to acquire a taste for alcohol.

Jesse decided to tackle her future father-in-law head on. "Mr Bolton, I can understand that you are concerned about Joshua marrying someone you barely know. And I am certain that he marrying someone from a different country makes matters worse." "Oh no!" he exclaimed feebly. "Please don't think that you are not welcome in this family. It's just that we don't know anything about you," he added apologetically. "And I told you that you would get to know Jesse better in due time!" came an icy response from the door. Joshua strode into the room taking both Jesse and his father by surprise. "I will not! I repeat, I will not allow anyone to speak to my future wife like that! How dare you ask Jesse if she had a drinking problem?" he boomed. "Calm down Joshua. It's all right. I can understand your father's concern," she soothed him. Jesse stood up and put her arm around Josh's waist. She could see his blood pulsating in his jaw. "It's okay! Really, Josh. Perhaps I should have an opportunity to speak alone with your parents then they can ask me all the questions that they want. It will put their hearts and minds at rest." Her conciliatory tone put Josh at ease but he wasn't going to allow his father to dictate whom he was going to marry - not this time! Josh was very angry and embarrassed at his father's behaviour. Jesse's family had been so welcoming and accepting of him. He wanted her to have a similar experience with his family.

Mrs Bolton appeared in the doorway smiling. "Come everybody, dinner is served." She could see that her son was upset and had no doubt in her mind who was the cause of it. As they walked into the dining room, she spoke rapid Italian to her son. He responded in Italian as well. It was the first time that Jesse had heard Josh speaking another language. She looked surprised at him and decided to change the subject. "So, how was the horse riding?" Josh turned his attention to her. "It was great love. I had no idea I missed horse riding so much," he beamed. "Bodmin moor is as beautiful as ever." "Blackbird took to Josh in an instant," added Nico excitedly. "Josh had a chance to ride in the new tack." Jesse could see that he was really glad to have his brother back. "I don't know why I didn't think of getting horses for *Sonder Moeite*," he questioned himself. "That's because it's a wine farm Josh, not an equestrian farm," she laughed. They all looked at Jesse and laughed. Her laughter was contagious and had definitely broken the iciness of the past moment. Looking at her, Josh confirmed, "I'm going to buy you a horse when we get back home. You have no idea how thrilling it can be, with the wind in your hair and your feet off the ground, you'll feel as though you are flying," he looked longingly at her. "Well in that case I have to come to *Sonder Moeite* too," chipped in Nico, pronouncing the words *Sonder Moeite* quite incorrectly. "Someone has to look after the horse," he laughed. Jesse noticed that Mrs Bolton had winced when Josh called *Sonder Moeite* 'home'. In a strange way, she felt sorry for her.

Two days later Jesse had her conversation with Mr and Mrs Bolton. Mrs Bolton seemed very embarrassed by Mr Bolton's questions. But no doubt, she was also relieved at the answers Jesse gave. It gave them both an opportunity to get to know her better. "I can't believe you've never met your own father," stated Mr Bolton snr. "If you want me to help track him down, I have friends in Intelligence," he stated quite seriously. "That won't be necessary Mr Bolton. I wouldn't want to drag him to the party kicking and screaming. No doubt he already has his own life and his own family." Jesse felt that her father had abandoned her a long time ago. It would be foolhardy to expect him to resume responsibility at this late stage of their lives and besides he might see her as an intrusion in his life.

That night Mr Bolton tossed and turned. Eventually he sat up in bed and woke his wife. "What kind of man, abandons a precious little girl like Jesse," he wrung his fingers in anger. Gina, I tell you that girl looks too familiar. I've seen her somewhere but where?" he wracked his brain. "Well Andrew she did say that she came to London to look for her father a few years ago," Gina said comfortingly. She could see that her husband wanted to protect Jesse and his way of doing this was getting to the root of the problem. "No, no! I haven't seen her before. I've seen someone who looks like her. But whom?" Mr Bolton was exasperated. Eventually husband and wife both fell asleep.

Jesse and Josh were up early the next morning. He was determined to devote more time to his bride to be. In fact, he felt very embarrassed about his father's behaviour. "I'm sorry babe; I won't allow anyone to disrespect you. He pulled her close to him. Jesse could see into the depths of his eyes. "I promise to look after you until the end of my days," he said quietly. "And I you," she promised. Their eyes locked and he slowly lowered his lips to hers. He kissed her deeply, passionately. He took her beautiful face in his strong hands and said "I love you" in Italian. "Feel free to say that again," she smiled. "I love you Jesse Kearns and I promise to make you infinitely happy." Jesse felt warm and protected. The love that Josh had for her would certainly make up for the love that she didn't receive from her father.

Josh spent the next few days showing Jesse around Bodmin and the rest of Cornwall. He took her to the town and they spent a considerable amount of time at the market. Jesse bought a few antique ornaments for her new home in South Africa. Josh took her on long drives in the country and some evenings they would go to a pub to have some traditional English food and listen to the stories of the locals. When they were not, out driving about, they remained on the estate and Josh tried to get Jesse to go horse riding with him. She refused and was too afraid because she had heard many stories about riders being thrown from their horses. She had had enough trouble with bicycles and she wasn't going to make a fool of herself on a horse. Cornwall presented an idyllic lifestyle and Jesse could see herself getting used to this way of life. But it would only suit her one day if she retired entirely from journalism and became a novelist. Her stay at Bodmin was very pleasant. Gina Bolton was the perfect hostess but Jesse couldn't say the same for Andrew Bolton. Something about him kept her on her guard.

Chapter 15

Josh's parents were adamant that they wanted to give Josh and his fiancée an engagement party. Josh suspected that his mother was merely looking for an excuse to have a social gathering. Gina Bolton loved entertaining and having people over to her home. This didn't happen often since she had moved to England. However, in Italy whenever she hosted a function at her family home the entire neighbourhood would come. Gina missed those days and she was not about to let Josh take this opportunity away from her. "Are you sure you don't mind all these people," worried Josh. "I'll be fine Joshua. Your mother is just trying to show us that she cares about us. But just make sure you remain close by my side on Saturday night," she warned. "I won't let you out of my sight," confirmed Josh. It was settled then. The Bolton's were throwing a huge engagement party for Josh and Jesse.

Mr Bolton snr summoned Josh to the library early that morning. They had a long discussion regarding Jesse's future with Josh. Mr Bolton pointed out to Josh the importance of knowing who one's parents were. Their voices grew louder and louder as the older Bolton were trying to convince the other of his way of thinking. Eventually Josh stormed out of the library angry as hell. At that precise moment, Jesse was coming down the winding staircase. "Oh Josh! There you are!" she exclaimed. He did not look at her but marched out of the front door slamming it behind him and walked towards the stables. His behaviour took her by complete surprise.

Mrs Bolton spent the week organizing, purchasing, rearranging and planning for the momentous occasion. She had invitations that needed to be sent out, flowers that needed to be arranged, caterers that needed to be contacted, a band that needed to be hired but most importantly she was only going to be using *Sonder Moeite* wines at the engagement party. She was so proud of her son that she needed an opportunity to show off his success to the world. Mrs Bolton tried to include Jesse in all the arrangements but Jesse knew that it was mostly for her own sake. She didn't mind at all. Mrs Bolton was very kind and generous and it was a good opportunity for the family to get together again. Gina went shopping with Josh and Jesse for new outfits. She was so excited she could scream. Josh insisted on khaki pants and a navy blazer. He had no intentions of being a stiff Brit all evening. He wanted to be as casual as possible. It seemed that some South African customs had rubbed off onto him already. He looked so suave standing in front of the mirror with his hands in his pockets. However, strangely enough Jesse could see that he was making a half hearted attempt to be happy. Ever since she had seen him storm out of the library, she noticed that his attitude towards her had changed. She couldn't understand what the matter could be. Jesse wanted to ask but she didn't want to cause a scene in front of his mother. Perhaps she would have an opportunity to speak to him later. Jesse settled on a midnight blue halter neck dress with a sprinkling of Swarovski crystals down the side of the dress. Mrs Bolton insisted that they both model in front of the mirror at the exclusive boutique. Josh loved to indulge his mother so he and Jesse pretended to be experienced models on the catwalk. This delighted her and she squealed with laughter clapping her hands. Not even she noticed the strain between them. He was clearly putting on a show to please his mother but unfortunately, Jesse could see right through him. That strange look he wore in his eyes in Cape Town had returned. She also noticed that Josh avoided contact with her. His attitude had become brusque and cold.

Jesse wondered what was going on. Ever since their arrival in Cornwall, Mr Bolton seemed to be trying to break up their relationship. She remembered once that Josh had mentioned that his father was prejudiced against people who were not pure British, even though his wife was Italian. Jesse's problem was that not only was she not pure British but she was an illegitimate half-breed as well. This made matters worse for her. Jesse's mind was going crazy.

120

Perhaps Mr Bolton had convinced Josh not to marry her after all. He may have wanted to preserve the bloodline. She couldn't believe that in this day and age people could still think like that. On the other hand, perhaps he preferred the mighty rich Ava for his son. In the car on the way home, Mrs Bolton sensed the tension between her son and her future daughter-in-law but she said nothing. As soon as they got back from shopping, Jesse went to her room.

She threw her packages on the floor near the Georgian styled wardrobes and flung herself on the bed. Her mind was racing. Josh's behaviour didn't make any sense to her. He had barely spoken a word to her all morning and avoided any physical or eye contact with her. Perhaps he had succumbed to his father's wishes or perhaps he was getting cold feet. Would she ever fit into his world? Her mother had raised her to have dignity and pride and if Joshua Bolton didn't want her, she would simply go back to Cape Town. It had happened before. She had enough pride and dignity not to throw herself at him. By now, Jesse was really troubled and determined to confront Josh.

Later that morning, Jesse strode out towards the stable looking for Josh. She found him with Blackbird. He was grooming the horse and looked up as she entered. "Josh, I need to talk to you," she pleaded. "I'm about to go riding," he said coldly. "Well, what I have to say can't wait," Jesse returned icily. "Your attitude towards me has changed."

"Really," he sneered. "And what has brought you to that brilliant conclusion?" The sarcasm in his voice made her wince. "Don't be a coward Joshua! If you don't want to marry me, I'll simply return to Cape Town."

"My mother has already made most of the preparations for the party and neither you nor I are going to disappoint her!" With those words he brushed past her, taking Blackbird by the reigns and walking out of the stable and into the sunshine, leaving her to stare at his back.

Poor Jesse was astounded. She didn't realize the hold that Josh's father had over him. Only now did she begin to understand the meaning of 'power' and 'money'. However, she couldn't punish Gina Bolton by pulling out of the engagement party. Gina had put in such a lot of effort already, not to mention the amount of money she had already spent on the party. Jesse would attend the engagement party and once she was in Cape Town she would break off the engagement. It was the only way she knew how to handle this situation. She felt that she was betraying Gina Bolton, who only had good intentions. Jesse was heartbroken. She needed her own mother at a time like this. Everything seemed so rosy before she came to England. Now she would have to return to her old life, all her dreams shattered. It was no use; Joshua Bolton was an immature man who was easily swayed by prestige and the power of his father.

The big night subsequently arrived. Guests streamed into the grey marbled hallway. Waiters hurried about serving cocktails and *Sonder Moeite* wine, while the band played light fusion jazz in the background. A hush fell over the crowd as Mrs Bolton introduced the band, telling the crowd that they would play Josh and Jesse's favourite song. Then Mr Bolton announced the couple with a lot of pomp and ceremony, "Ladies and gentlemen, I'd like to introduce my eldest son Joshua Bolton and his bride to be, Jesse Kearns. This entire charade reminded Jesse of the Middle Eastern guests that she had entertained in Cape Town. The pretentiousness was just a bit much. The couple came walking slowly down the mahogany and brass molded staircase, Jesse reached unconsciously for Josh's hand and he held hers firmly in his but his hand felt cold and detached. The chemistry between them was gone. 'Who was this stranger?' thought Jesse. She continued like a robot down the stairs, her legs moving forward without any feeling.

Josh thought that his mother was crazy. She behaved as though they were royalty. Jesse could hear the 'oohs' and 'aahs' coming from the gathering at the foot of the stairs. Many people congratulated them. Jesse couldn't remember half the names that were introduced to her; her mind being somewhere else. Jesse worried that Ava would appear amongst the crowd and that Josh would not protect her against his powerful ex-wife. She looked about half expecting to hear Ava's shrill laughter across the crowded room. Josh introduced Jesse to many people – but most of the names, she did not remember.

The band played a traditional Cape Town jazz song and Jesse longed to dance. 'I might as well try to enjoy tonight,' she comforted herself. She also had to give Gina the impression that she was enjoying herself and that she appreciated her efforts. Jesse took Josh's hand and pulled him onto the dance floor. They danced the jazz, which is very similar to a mixture between the salsa and the samba. When Josh came to Cape Town it was one of the first things he had learned. In fact, he knew he had to learn to dance Cape Town style in order to integrate with the community. However, his Italian blood also helped in this endeavour. The crowd moved back while the couple of the evening expertly moved to sounds of the melody. People were awestruck when Josh swung and turned Jesse multiple times so that her dress lifted and her long slender legs were visible. When the song subsided, there was a roar of clapping and cheering. Jesse was breathless, her bosom heaving from the excitement of the dance. But nobody knew how her heart felt.

She had just sipped some juice when a tall man asked her to dance the waltz with him. She accepted. He was tall suave looking and possibly in his early fifties. He looked strangely familiar and made small talk with her while they danced. He was a well-traveled horse breeder and trainer. The only place he had not yet visited was Cape Town. He enquired after Jesse's educational background and the

123

circumstances under which she had met Joshua. Jesse told him about her formative years in Namibia, also how she had come to Cape Town. When she mentioned the word 'Namibia', she distinctly saw one of his eyebrows lifting in surprise. However, Jesse paid no heed to this. The dance ended and he returned her to Josh's side. Josh had a smile plastered to his face but his eyes once again revealed his troubled mind.

Jesse danced with many people that night. She couldn't remember all the names and faces and her head began to swirl with a mixture of excitement and dread. Hired staff started ushering guests towards a large adjoining dining room, decorated with white and green flowers and white lace ribbons. The long table had beautiful white linen tablecloths and white serviettes with green satin bordering. The finest china and silverware graced the long oak table. The food was a mixture of British, Italian and South African. When Jesse saw the koeksisters and breyani she felt slightly homesick. Gina Bolton had really gone the extra mile to make her feel welcome. It was a pity that all of this would eventually be in vain. The music tempo slowed down as people found their reserved seats. Mr Bolton made a speech, congratulating the couple and welcoming Jesse into the family. 'How false could a man really be,' thought Jesse? Mrs Bolton said a short prayer in Italian, as she was a staunch Roman Catholic. After the toast, the guests began to eat. Josh came to rescue Jesse from some elderly aunt and said she had better eat to maintain her strength. She couldn't understand why he even pretended to be concerned about her. He looked slightly pale though and she noticed a strained expression in his hazel eyes. Jesse thought it was the strain of so many people and having to put up a pretense for everyone. They ate partly in silence. A waiter came to whisper something in Josh's ear. When Jesse had finished eating, Josh excused himself and walked towards the library. After dinner the music and dancing continued. By twelve o'clock people started leaving and the family were all relieved because by now, everybody had had their fill of enjoyment and the tiredness began to set in.

Once the last guest had left, Jesse thanked the Bolton's and Josh walked her to her room. "Thank you." said Jesse lamely. "I'll see you in the morning. Sleep tight." He kissed her very briefly on her forehead before walking away. Josh had confirmed Jesse's puzzlement. There was no doubt his feelings for her had died. Imagine Josh kissing her on the forehead! They appeared like an old married couple with no sparks between them. Something didn't seem right with Josh. Not only was he distant and cold towards her but he seemed worried at the same time. She lay in bed wondering if he was having second thoughts about marrying her or if he doubted his decision to divorce Ava. Perhaps his father did after all have something to do with changing his mind. Eventually exhaustion took over and she fell soundly asleep.

Jesse dreamed again that she was walking across a meadow on the Bolton estate. She saw a man in the distance and as he passed, he raised one of his eyebrows ever so slightly. Jesse recognized him as the man she had danced with earlier that evening. She turned to call after him but he had already disappeared. She felt filled with a feeling of emptiness and rejection and continued walking across the meadow. Jesse woke up the next morning feeling tired and gloomy. She didn't have the energy to get out of bed and face the family.

Chapter 16

Finally, when she fully awoke she realized that she was not in her own home. Jesse turned to get up and saw an envelope on her nightstand. Her name appeared on the front in a very familiar handwriting - Josh's handwriting. She opened the envelope and it read, *'Gone to London on business. Josh.'* That was all. There was no 'love Josh' at the end. The note confirmed Jesse's suspicions. It seemed that Josh's feelings had changed. Jesse could not make head or tail of the note. What business had he in London? Was it business regarding the farm or was it business regarding the Bolton estate? Then it dawned on her that some time back Josh had mentioned that Ava was living in London. Why on earth would he be going to London, she wondered? And why hadn't he mentioned anything to her? Why was it such a big secret? Did Josh have unfinished business with Ava? She couldn't stand the uncertainty any longer. Jesse got up to shower. She stood under the warm pressure of the rain forest shower, allowing it to beat down on her as if it were massaging her back. She remembered her shower with Josh at *Sonder Moeite*. Her body ached for him and her breasts became hard and wanton as if seeking the lips of her lover. Beads of water cascaded over her bosom where Josh liked to nuzzle and kiss her. She caressed herself knowing that her hopes and dreams with Joshua Bolton would not come to pass. She doubted very much whether she would ever again know the sexual pleasure and affection that she had experienced with Josh.

After she got dressed, she came down to the breakfast room. An English breakfast filled the sideboard. She had no appetite at all but lifted the lids of the silver dishes anyway and dished some scrambled eggs and toast for herself, purely out of habit. Jesse felt sick to her stomach and felt like crawling back into bed but she knew that Gina Bolton would probably like to discuss the success of the previous evening. She didn't know how long she could keep up with this pretense.

As soon as she had finished her breakfast, Jesse tapped lightly on the heavy library doors and let herself in. She knew that Mr and Mrs Bolton would be sitting and having their tea there. As she opened the door, Mr Bolton stood leaning against the mantelpiece of the dominating mosaic stone fireplace with a grave expression on his face. She had a feeling that they were discussing her but she could not gleam much from his expression. "Good morning everyone," greeted Jesse as cheerily as she could muster. She walked over to Gina Bolton and pecked her on the cheek. "Thank you so much for last night Gina. It was wonderful!" said Jesse trying to hide her sadness. They both looked grave. "What is it?" asked Jesse perturbed? Mr Bolton stepped forward and said as calmly as possible, "Jesse, do you remember the tall man you danced with last night?" Jesse felt a sick feeling creeping into the pit of her stomach. "Had he died? Had something happened to him? Was it something to do with Josh having to go to London?"

"Yes. Has something happened to him? Is Joshua okay?" she asked concerned. "No, no, nothing of the sought," interjected Mr Bolton. "And Josh is fine" "Jesse, we have some difficult news for you," cautioned Gina. "Will someone please tell me what is going on?" she pleaded. She couldn't understand what the connection was with the man she had danced with last night. In fact, she had danced with many people. But her sixth sense told her that she was about to receive some foreboding news. They were silent at first. "If you don't want Joshua to marry me, its ok," she uttered desperately. "I'll go back to Cape Town as soon as possible." Tears were forming at the corners of her smoky eyes. Jesse envisaged the quiet before the storm. Mr Bolton seemed unusually gentle and caring. "What on earth are you talking about?" exclaimed Mr Bolton. "I'm aware that matters have changed between Josh and me," she muttered candidly.

"My dear, you have completely misunderstood the situation," he assured her.

To what situation was Mr Bolton referring? Why did Josh have to leave for London? Mr Bolton stepped forward and began to explain. "Jesse, please don't be angry," he started… "What is going on?" she begged. "Allow me to explain. Joshua mentioned your father to me when we had a meeting yesterday morning. He mentioned that the night that he met your mother she had asked him to protect you because your own father had let you down. Josh gave her his word." Jesse seemed surprised at this revelation. "Well, I seem to be talking in circles. Here," he handed her an envelope. Jesse opened it and there was a letter, half of which had been blanked out with a black Koki pen. There was only one paragraph that she could read. It read, 'I knew since our second meeting that the subject of your father was a very sensitive and painful one for you. I did not wish to mention him again and conjure up all the hurt from your past. On the other hand my father couldn't find his peace until he knew who your father was.' "Why is Josh saying this?" asked Jesse even more confused. "I have friends in the Intelligence Service and they were kind enough to investigate his whereabouts for us," informed Mr Bolton. "This is part of a brief from Intelligence, hence the rest of it being blanked out." Jesse's mind was spinning by know. 'Were they saying that they knew who her father was?' "The Colonel leading the investigation agreed that it would be best for Josh to distance himself from you while the investigation was under way," added Mr Bolton. "Why?" Jesse asked perturbed. "They didn't want to get your hopes up and secondly, Josh told me that after the way you spoke of British men in Africa we didn't know if you'd approve of the search and thirdly when dealing with the Intelligence Service everything has got to be confidential. We couldn't risk any information being leaked. Not even Gina knew what was going on," confirmed Mr Bolton.

"So have you found my father?" asked Jesse expectantly. "As yet we have not had word from Intelligence. That is why Josh traveled to London early this morning to determine if any information had come to pass. I informed him that since late this morning the situation had changed but he opted to continue his journey there in order to handle personal business matters. "What has changed?" asked Jesse even more confused. "Well, just after breakfast Bill Horner stepped forward and claims that he is your father, Jesse," answered Mr Bolton. "Who is Bill Horner?" "After the party last night, Bill came to me and mentioned that he had something very serious he wished to discuss with me this morning. He confessed that he might be your father," answered Mr Bolton. "He is the tall man you danced with last night." Gina had her arm around Jesse now and she felt the shiver of shock going through her petite body. Her head spun as she heard the words father. Suddenly she remembered her past few dreams and made the connections. She remembered that the man in her dream looked oddly familiar but she couldn't place him. Then she recognized the incident where the man she had danced with had lifted his eyebrow when she mentioned that she had spent her formative years in Namibia and the man she had dreamt of had also lifted his eyebrow. They were the same person. Could he be her father? The photograph she carried around with her was of a man about twenty-five years younger. She turned to Gina, "I'll go and fetch the photograph to make sure." With that, she spun around and ran out of the library. Jesse wasn't sure what to feel. Her head was spinning but excitement was rising out of her belly. She came flying down the broad staircase with photograph in hand. Gina took the photo calmly from her. The resemblance between the young man and the man that Jesse had danced with was very strong. "Oh Lord! I can't believe I've found my father." "Calm down dear, calm down," cooed Gina Bolton. She placed a cup of tea in Jesse's trembling hands and told her to breathe deeply. "Bill has asked – I mean William Horner has asked to meet with you Jesse," continued Mr. Bolton. "Jesse you don't have to meet him if you don't want to," stated Gina firmly. Jesse wished that Josh were here now. He would protect her from this runaway father who after twenty-four years wanted to make his acquaintance with his daughter. Mr Bolton could not imagine a father running away from a child like Jesse and he felt deeply sorry for her. "Are you sure you are up to this?" asked Gina worriedly. "I have waited for twenty four years to meet him. I think it's long overdue," she said softly. Jesse's large almond shaped child-like eyes looked lost. She wanted Josh here with her. But she didn't know how he felt about her. He was so cold and distant now. And why did he have to continue his journey to London knowing that her father was right here? She knew she couldn't ask his parents about his reason for going to London. Now was not the time to discuss her differences with Josh. "Gina, will you and Mr Bolton stay with me when he comes?" she pleaded. "Of course we'll be here. We won't let anything happen to you Jesse," she said pulling her closer. Her body seemed to flutter in anticipation. Both Gina and Andrew Bolton realized that they deeply loved their future daughter-in-law. They would do anything to protect her as if she were their own child.

A meeting was arranged for later that morning. Mr Bolton called Bill Horner and told him that Jesse had agreed to meet with him. There was tension in the air. Jesse sat on her bed with her hands under her thighs. She stared at the floor. A myriad of thoughts penetrated her mind. 'What if he didn't like her? What would happen if she didn't like him? What would she do if he didn't fulfill the fantasy she had created about who he was and why he had left her? She couldn't believe that she had already danced with her own father. Jesse tried to console herself. 'Everything will be okay. Just don't have any expectations, that way you won't be disappointed.' This entire situation is unreal. 'I've waited for this moment all my life. I have created so many movies in my head regarding this meeting.'

Jesse used to manipulate the endings based on her mood. When she was sad she'd have a sad ending to her fantasy movie. When she was happy, she'd have a happy ending to her fantasy movie. Now that it had become a reality, she didn't have a clue as to what to say to him or how to behave towards him. She tried to imagine what her grandmother would say. Jesse could almost hear her. *'All you need to do my love is to be Jesse. You don't have to explain yourself or apologize for who you are. Let him do the talking. He screwed up, let him fix this.'* She would do what her grandmother would have done. She took comfort in her grandmother's teachings and the pressure of the moment somehow lifted. She longed for Josh now and wished that he were here now to help her with this situation. He would have said all the right things at a time like this. She needed him at one of the most important moments of her life. But by now, he was probably in Ava's arms.

Jesse walked alone down the mahogany and brass molded staircase to the library. She felt apprehensive as her feet sunk into the plush violet carpet. She could hear voices as she approached. The time had come for Jesse to meet her father. As she stood in front of the library door, Jesse braced herself. 'It's all right,' she said to herself, 'just take a deep breath and relax.' Jesse smiled and took a deep breathe. She exhaled slowly as she opened the heavy library door. Mr Bolton and a tall man stood up as Jesse entered the library. The man was William Horner. His eyes fixed on Jesse. He stepped forward and introduced himself. "William Horner, you can call me Bill," he indicated stretching out his hand. "Jesse Kearns," she promptly stuck out her hand to meet his. The air was tense and Mrs Bolton offered to pour tea. There was silence as she poured and handed each one a delicate periwinkle porcelain cup. Jesse eyed Bill Horner under her long lashes. He was tall and lanky. Bill had a lovely tan. There was no doubt that he had spent a considerable amount of time in Africa. His hair was long and sun bleached. He had a wide mouth, which looked strangely familiar. There was something very pleasing about him. Jesse could see why her mother had fallen for him.

Her beauty mesmerized him. She reminded him of Rebecca. "You have your mother's beautiful eyes," he uttered quite surprised. Jesse smiled not knowing if she should say 'thank you' for the compliment or not. She wanted to ask him many questions but didn't know how to start. Should she just be blunt and ask him why he had left her mother with a small baby. "But Jesse has your mouth, Bill," proclaimed Mrs Bolton purposefully. "Quite so, quite so my dear," he agreed. The situation seemed more than agreeable and Andrew Bolton discreetly suggested, "Perhaps we should leave Jesse and Bill to catch up. Mrs Bolton agreed and stood up to leave. "If you don't mind I'd prefer it if you both stayed." Jesse's eyes were almost begging them. They both resumed their seats. "You don't mind if we stay, do you Bill?" challenged Gina knowing that her family paid the man his salary every month. "Not at all," he answered uncomfortably. Jesse thought that it was no use getting his back up against the wall, the damage of all the years of absence had already been done.

An uncomfortable silence ensued. Jesse was determined not to be the first to speak. Bill leaned forward and said, "I'm sure you have many questions you'd like to ask, Jesse?"
Mr Bolton leaned forward too, "Bill, it was you who called this meeting. Why don't you fire away," he suggested doing his best to try and protect Jesse. "You're right, I did call this meeting. When I saw you dancing with Josh at the engagement party, my head spun as I laid eyes on you. I saw Rebecca again twenty-five years ago. I knew I couldn't be wrong because I have only seen one such beauty in my lifetime." He sighed and the faraway look in his eyes made Jesse almost feel sorry for him. "I was young and foolish Jesse. I was engaged to my childhood sweetheart at the time. I became very confused and thought that coming to Africa would clear my head and give me a sense of direction. I fell in love with your mother. It was a torrid romance. I knew that I'd have to go back to England at some point and I was torn between the love of my life, Rebecca and my

dearest friend Mary. When I heard that Rebecca was pregnant, I was really scared but we had the most beautiful baby girl together. I named you Jesse after my childhood pet dog, Jessica," he uttered mournfully. "You named me after a dog?"

"It wasn't like that at all," protested Bill. Jesse thought that if Josh had been here he would have secretly laughed. Mr Bolton looked slightly amused. Then Gina uttered indignantly, "Well I hope at least that it was a beautiful dog!" Then Jesse started laughing when she saw how ridiculous her naming sounded. "It's not funny," she gasped, "I was named after a dog!" They all laughed when Bill realized the humour in her statement. The ice was broken by now and everybody seemed more relaxed.

You were almost a year old when Mary became gravely ill. I rushed back to England to be at her side. We had promised to marry each other when we were both twenty-one years old. I felt that I had betrayed Mary and that God was punishing me by making Mary ill. When Mary recovered, I married her immediately. We were married for fifteen years without any children. Mary couldn't have children. With every year that went by, we grew more and more distant. I couldn't make her happy. Mary passed away nine years ago. I thought that marrying her would fill the void but her death accentuated it even more. After her death, I thought I would have an opportunity to reconnect with Rebecca. I tried searching for her but there was no trace of Rebecca in Namibia. Some people mentioned that she was living in South Africa but knew nothing of her whereabouts."

Jesse didn't know what to say. The story was indeed sad. But her mother had to suffer in the process. She had to suffer - growing up without a father. "That sounds like a very sad story," retorted Jesse lamely. "Are you expecting sympathy from Jesse, Bill?" questioned

Mr Bolton candidly. "Andrew, I screwed up three beautiful women's lives. I am not looking for sympathy. I hold myself responsible."

"Did you ever even think about me?" asked Jesse pensively. "Jesse, I have thought of you every day for the last twenty four years, I wish I had done things differently back then. I was young and stupid. I loved your mother with all my heart but I couldn't disappoint Mary. We have all paid the price for my choices and I am truly sorry. I wish I was a better man," whispered Bill painfully.

Andrew Bolton could sense that Bill was not putting on a show. He could sense that Bill had also suffered a lot of heartache being separated from a woman that he truly loved and the circumstances were such that his situation seemed to have spiraled out of control. Bill leaned forward as if to beg Jesse for her understanding. "Jesse you must understand that with every year that went by, it became more and more difficult to go back. I know that this is not what you want to hear but being without you and your mother has been a very lonely experience for me. I've missed out on so much. And you could have taught me so many things too. I hope that one day you can forgive me?"

Jesse leaned back in her seat on the green brocade sofa. She smiled and thought to herself that it was no use being angry or trying to punish this man. He had already punished himself. She was also grateful that her mother and grandmother had raised her. Because of their influence and teaching, she had become the woman she is today: intelligent, patient and understanding but above all compassionate and kind. Jesse would not have changed that for the entire world. Bill had truly punished himself. He had missed out on great family experiences with her and her mother and grandmother. Jesse believed that one day he would have to answer for his deeds and if she continued to punish him by being bitter or resentful, then the cycle would simply continue. It was not worth it.

Jesse stood up to Gina's surprise. "Bill you did the best that you could with the knowledge and emotional maturity you had at the time. I'm not going to gain anything by punishing you further. So if you're willing, I'm willing to start again too." Bill stood up as well and there was a moment of awkwardness. Jesse made the first move by stretching out her arms. Tears flowed down Bill's face as he embraced his daughter for the first time in twenty-four years. Even Mr Bolton had a lump in his throat. He looked away and cleared his throat hoping that no one had seen his emotions well up inside of him.

There's just one thing I'd like from you," asked Jesse candidly. "Anything, anything at all my dear," assured Bill. "You're my father and it feels weird calling you 'Bill'," she posed. "Well, perhaps err…," stuttered Bill. "Yes Bill what do you suggest," mocked Gina. "I err…" he trailed off in mid sentence. Jesse could see from whom Josh inherited his sense of humour. All three of them were looking at him waiting for an answer. They all burst out laughing. Seeing Bill squirm was a mixture of awkwardness and fun for them. "Don't be so serious old chap!" joked Andrew Bolton, slapping him on the back. "Well, when you were a baby I used to say you were Papa's little girl," he answered shyly.

"I call my mother Mama and it makes sense to call my father Papa. Okay, Papa it is then," she agreed. "Just don't expect Josh to call you Papa when they're married," warned Andrew Bolton. Bill had a glint in his eye and said, "I know that Josh will really keep me on my toes. I should ask him if it's tradition for the groom to be, to ask the father's permission for his daughter's hand in marriage." Bill said dryly. "And we all know what Josh's response to that will be," laughed Gina. Gina enjoyed ragging Bill but secretly she wanted to hurt him back for hurting this innocent child.

A lot had happened in such a short space of time. Meeting Josh's family, the so-called misunderstanding between Josh and Jesse, which had not been entirely cleared up yet, then there was the engagement party and all the talk of the wedding preparations and now meeting her father. By now, Jesse was emotionally drained. Mrs Bolton had arranged for them to have a family dinner that night. Of course, Bill Horner was also invited, so that he and his long lost daughter could continue to reconnect. After the intensity of the meeting that morning, Bill and Mr Bolton went to the stables to take care of riders in the up and coming show jumping competition. Mrs Bolton insisted that Jesse go and have a nap. Jesse instead opted to go for a walk in the meadows. She was grateful for this brief interlude. She needed to absorb, reflect on and process the day's events. As Jesse picked some pretty daisies to plait a crown for herself, she thought about who her father had turned out to be. She couldn't believe that she had found him right on her future parents-in-law's doorstep after the years of searching and wondering. Fate had dealt her an even hand. A new relationship lay ahead of her; a father-daughter relationship. It seemed that this relationship might even replace her relationship with Josh. She thought that she had found a partner who was willing to share everything with her and a man she could look up to, respect and challenge. Mr Bolton had said that what happened between her and Josh was simply a misunderstanding. But why was he not here with her now? What reason did he have to be in London? Except for Ava... If Josh had decided that his life was with Ava, well then Jesse didn't know how she would pick up the pieces again. She didn't even know if Josh would tell her the truth. He had withheld information from her in the past. It was difficult for her to understand him when every now and then he blew hot and cold at the same time. If she felt this unsure about Joshua, she would not be able to give one hundred percent of herself again – to anybody. Jesse could only hope that this really was a misunderstanding.

In spite of everything, finding her father was more than she had ever hoped could happen. Jesse was very grateful for this. Life had turned out unexpectedly well. Now it was only Joshua who had to sort himself out. These exciting and crazy thoughts continued to mull about in her head. 'What would Mama say if she knew that I had just met my father?' thought Jesse. Her mother never ever mentioned her father's name. Jesse knew that it was painful for her and that she had tried all those years to put it behind her. She knew that she would be opening up old wounds again by telling her mother about her meeting with Bill Horner. But then again there were no secrets between Jesse and her mother. Rebecca Kearns has always known how much it meant for Jesse to find her father. Jesse thought it best for her to tell her mother in person.

Dinner was extremely pleasant later that evening. But Josh was not there. His family presumed that he would return the next day. The only problem was that the next day was the day they were to return to South Africa. Dinner was delightful, but she missed Josh's presence at the table and the empty chair next to Jesse reminded her of a love so great that her heart could not fathom losing it. Mrs Bolton indulged everyone again with a scrumptious dinner. The family sat in the family dining room. It was cozy yet elegant with long candelabra's in the middle of the table stuffed with pink and white flowers flowing between the lit candles. Mrs Bolton took pride in her decorative abilities and ensured that her staff had used the best silver and porcelain. She used one of her most expensive hand embroidered lace tablecloths with matching serviettes from Italy. The table setting was very pretty. Tonight she opted for traditional English cuisine. They had herring soup with cottage pie and Yorkshire pudding. Mrs Bolton felt that Jesse reconnecting with her father after so many years was something truly worth celebrating. There was a lot of amusing banter around the table and every so often Jesse caught her father looking at her. She could see the unmistakable admiration he had in his eyes. Her heart warmed over and she felt that she had finally found her place in the world. After dinner, Mrs Bolton insisted that Jesse and Bill take a walk in the meadows. She felt that it was important for the two of them to have a little privacy before the couple flew back to South Africa.

Bill was very glad for this opportunity to get to know his only child better. They strolled out of the large house, down the marbled steps of the pillared patio and down a gravel lane until they got to the meadows. It was green and peaceful - tiny white and yellow daisies were scattered here and there. One meadow seemed to roll into another before them. As they walked, Bill told Jesse about his travels to Africa as a young man. How he had met Rebecca at a charity dance knowing that she was the one. He told her about their first year together. "You were the most beautiful baby I had ever seen," he said reaching out to hold her hand. His hand was warm and strong in hers and Jesse felt instantly safe and protected by her father. She instinctively knew that he wouldn't allow anything bad to happen to her. "Papa, everybody thinks that their child is the most beautiful child in the world," she laughed. When Bill heard her call him Papa his eyes welled up with tears. He turned to her and held her face in his hard hands, "Jesse you have no idea how long I have waited to hear those words. The hole in my heart is finally closed." He embraced her, breathing deeply to smell her hair and her skin. He stepped back to look closely at her. "I'm sorry for all the pain that I have caused you and I promise that everyday I will try to be a better man and a good father to you."

"Things may not always be smooth sailing with us but I now know what you look like. I don't have to look at an old photograph of you. I can visit you and call you whenever I want to," she smiled contently. "You can call and visit me whenever you like," assured Bill. "And Jesse, Josh is a good man. I have no doubt that he will treat you with respect."

"But Papa, he isn't even here and we are meant to fly back tomorrow," she answered worriedly. "Don't worry, he'll come and what ever is worrying you now, just remember that Josh is an honorable man." She wanted to believe her father. They walked back to the house, as dusk was saying goodbye to the sky, holding hands as father and daughter reunited.

Jesse spent the next day doing last minute shopping before their evening flight back to South Africa. Josh arrived back from London just before lunch. And still he had not said anything to Jesse. She felt as though she was holding her breathe waiting for his bombshell. Mrs Bolton was in a flurry and in her typical Italian style, she wanted them to take so much with them; homemade pasta, wedding fabric and hand embroidered tablecloths she had made for the bridal couple. After a last family luncheon, Jesse and Josh packed their suitcases meticulously in order to make space for the extra goodies Mrs Bolton had put in for them. Josh insisted that his family do not come with them to the airport. He knew his mother would be a bundle of nerves and he couldn't take her tears. There were tearful goodbyes as their rented car stood in the winding driveway waiting for them. Mrs Bolton couldn't let go of her son. "Mama, the wedding is in six weeks time. We will see you soon," he consoled his mother. "Josh is right Gina and besides you are flying out two weeks before the wedding so you can help Jesse," Mr Bolton fruitlessly tried to console his dear wife as she rang her handkerchief in her hands. Josh and Jesse got into the rented car and waved goodbye as they drove down the winding gravel driveway. Mr and Mrs Bolton waved until they couldn't see them anymore. Jesse wondered if Josh was being sincere to his parents about the wedding still taking place.

Initially, Jesse did not speak to Josh on the way and he appeared to have a thousand things on his mind although he could sense the tension coming from his passenger. After they had driven out of town, He looked at her and said, "Penny for your thoughts?" She was silent for a few seconds before she answered him. "I am not the one who behaved so badly. I am not the one who disappeared to London without saying a word. So I don't have anything to say," she uttered scathingly. Josh was quiet for a moment as though he were gathering his thoughts together. He knew that he had to rectify the situation and it was going to be hard for him to make up to her for missing one of the most important moments of her life - Finding and reconciling with her father. "I am sorry I was not there for you when you needed me most. I thought that I was acting in your best interests. I followed the advice of the Intelligence guys but clearly it could have been handled better."

"Joshua, why didn't you just tell me that you were attempting to find my father?"

"Jesse initially I didn't want to get involved. It was my father who insisted on having his way. We had a huge argument as I thought he was meddling and would bring up old hurt feelings in you once more. Then again, it was the Intelligence guys who briefed me on how to conduct myself." Jesse could understand that the entire incident had come from a place of good intent. It was however, awkward to have such an intense conversation when Josh's mind was on the road and on the traffic. He wanted to turn to her and look her in the eye and say all the right things but at this stage all Josh could think of was that he and Jesse had come this far. He couldn't allow an incident conjured up by the Intelligence to come between him and his future wife. He liked the sound of those words – his future wife.

They arrived at Heathrow almost two and a half hours later. The airport was congested as usual, but somehow they managed to get to their terminal immediately and board their plane in record time. Jesse was grateful that Josh had booked them on business class tickets. When she had traveled to England as a young graduate, she could only afford economy class tickets. The luxury of business class made all the difference on such a long flight. Jesse decided that she needed to clear matters between them entirely before she landed in Cape Town. She did not want to start a life in Cape Town with loose threads or swords hanging over her. "Josh, why did you behave so coldly towards me?" she questioned candidly. "Like my father said the Intelligence Service wanted me to distance myself from you in case my relationship with you influenced their investigation." "How was your relationship with me going to influence the investigation?" asked Jesse confused and doubtful. "I know many important people, Jesse and perhaps they thought that I would use my influence during the investigation. However, I think that they were also simply following protocol," he concluded. She was only half-satisfied with his answer. She looked at him skeptically. "Believe me, I didn't want to hurt you. I wanted what was best for you – finding your father – at least I thought that finding him would make all the difference to you and the only way I knew how to distance myself from you was to be cold and distant. You have no idea how much I longed for you," he confessed. "You heard about Bill being my father before you got to London, why didn't you just come back?" she asked overtly. "Jesse, I thought I would kill two birds with one stone. I knew that my parents would take good care of you. They adore you. I had to purchase some equipment for the farm, which will be shipped to South Africa next week and I had to take care of a surprise for you as well. And now don't make me tell you what it is okay," he answered trying to diffuse her anger and her hurt. "Okay, but then just give me a hint," she questioned lightening up a bit. "Jesse Kearns, you are incorrigible. Okay, it's for the wedding day," he answered surreptitiously pressing the tiny box in his pocket with his hand just to make sure that it was still there. Jesse was relieved that Josh had not gone to London to see Ava. Her father was right - Josh was an honorable man. So her concerns about Josh's family not accepting her because of her mixed heritage were all unnecessary. She just heard from Josh's own lips that they adored her. This made her smile. Her concerns about Josh going back to Ava had simply been a waste of her time and energy. The mind can surely play tricks on the head and the heart when one is insecure. She knew from now on that Josh's past was exactly that – his past. Jesse snuggled next to Josh as the aeroplane taxied down the runway. Soon they were high above the clouds. Josh looked at her and said, "I can't wait for our lives to begin together at home at *Sonder Moeite*. I love you," he kissed her tenderly. Jesse's heart welled over with emotion. The time had come for her to marry Joshua Bolton, a man without whom she could not imagine her life. "I love you too Joshua. I can't wait to see the blue skies of Cape Town, to hear the birds sing at *Sonder Moeite* and to smell the wine fermenting in the vats. We are going to have a wonderful life together," she smiled, kissing him at the corner of his wicked dimple.

www.ingramcontent.com/pod-product-compliance
Lightning Source LLC
Chambersburg PA
CBHW070936130626
46555CB00001B/461